LEGACY

SISTERS OF WRATH

BOOK ONE

SIENNA SNOW

SISTERS OF WRATH
BOOK 1

LEGACY

by

Sienna Snow

Cover Design: Steamy Designs

Editor: Jennifer Haymore

www.siennasnow.com

ISBN - eBook - 979-8-88535-040-2

ISBN - Print - 979-8-88535-038-9

AI Disclosure

This work was written without the use of generative artificial intelligence (AI). The author strictly prohibits any organization from utilizing this publication to train AI technologies for text generation, including but not limited to technologies that can produce works in a similar style or genre as this publication.

Tropes List

- Dark Mafia
- Enemies to lovers
- Arranged marriage
- Forbidden love
- Villain romance
- Antihero
- Morally Gray Characters
- marriage of convenience
- Beauty and Beast dynamic
- Hate to love you
- Defiant submission
- Redemption arc
- Love-hate dynamic
- Revenge
- Forced proximity
- Possessive alpha hero
- Strong, defiant heroine

- Touch her and die
- Claiming and ownership
- Power couple dynamic
- Rival families
- Feuding families
- Dark secrets
- Hidden truths
- Mutual obsession
- Beauty as weapon
- Dangerous attraction
- Betrayal and redemption
- Damaged characters
- Tragic backstory
- Forced Trust

Author's Note
Content Warning

This book is a dark romance with subject matter
that may trigger some readers.

- Graphic Violence
- Explicit Sexual Content
- Dominance themes
- Kidnapping or Forced Marriage
- Dark Themes
- Morally Gray Characters
- Death & Loss
- Gaslighting & Psychological Manipulation
- Weapons & Violence
- Toxic relationships
- Manipulative behavior
- Emotional Abuse & Manipulation
- Coercive dynamics

- Trauma & PTSD
- Strong Language
- Forced Trust

ONE

No more waiting...

I longed to return to the land of my birth, the home my sisters and I had fled like thieves in the night. It was time to reclaim our rightful place at the seat of our family's power, and none of those who had wronged us would see it coming.

The mere thought of setting foot on Greek soil once again filled me with a rush of emotions, from anticipation and excitement to nervousness. But I couldn't afford to let impatience rule me. The only way to achieve our ultimate goal was to plan and execute each and every step carefully.

Despite the numerous tasks on my agenda, I knew that now was the time to set things in motion for the future we deserved. I had waited and watched for fifteen years, biding my time to finally serve justice to all who had betrayed us.

And now, as the last grains of sand trickled through the hourglass, I knew that the Vitalis family was ready for revenge.

But first, I needed to meet with the man who had sacrificed everything to keep us alive. I wanted to keep him in the loop about our plans out of respect for his unwavering loyalty and protection.

As I approached a busy intersection near Prague's old town, I brushed a stray hair from my forehead and paused to observe the bustling morning traffic. After waiting for a break in the cars, I crossed the street and headed toward one of my favorite cafes. I selected a table with a strategic view of anyone who approached the establishment. The server greeted me with a nod and served me my preferred morning brew without asking.

I had ten minutes until my formidable companion arrived. Inhaling deep, I relaxed and took in the sights around me. As pedestrians bustled by on their daily tasks, they would never suspect that the woman sitting in front of them was an impostor—someone who had learned their language at a young age and seamlessly blended into their society.

But it was all for my sisters, for the legacy that deserved better. I would do anything for them, even if it meant becoming a master of deception and shedding blood to bring justice for everything the bastards took from us on that fateful night.

As the server set my coffee down on the table, I welcomed

the warmth spreading through my fingers. In my youth, revenge had consumed my thoughts and clouded my judgment. But with time, I learned that rash actions only led to more chaos. And so, I waited patiently for the right moment to strike. Finally, it was upon us.

A surge of power and determination flowed through my veins. I had the means to retaliate against those who had ruthlessly ruined my life and my family. As I sat in the quaint section of the bustling café, sipping on freshly refilled coffee, I saw Vik Remes walk confidently down the sidewalk. Seeing him only solidified my resolve and the path I knew I must take.

As he drew closer, a sinking feeling settled in my gut. Speaking with him was the first step in executing my plan, and his support would make things significantly easier. However, I wasn't seeking his approval or validation. No one was the boss of me, and no one ever would be.

Despite this fact, out of respect for our history together, I felt it necessary to consult with Vik before making any major decisions that would impact our lives. A small smile tugged at my lips as he approached my table with his signature powerful stride.

Heads turned to catch a glimpse of the tall and distinguished man passing by. Younger women peered over their sunglasses while older ladies did double-takes, admiring his confidence and commanding presence. Vik wasn't flashy, but he exuded an aura of strength and cunning that was hard to ignore. It was a lesson he had drilled into me from the very beginning: true power didn't need to be flaunted or announced. It was something that spoke for itself through subtle gestures and mannerisms.

Vik's tan skin seemed to glow under the warm sun as he homed in on my face and sat across from me at the bistro table. The slight tightening of his jaw indicated that he hadn't anticipated my early arrival. He preferred others to feel as if they were the ones to arrive late in order to maintain an upper hand in any situation.

Vik prided himself on knowing me inside and out, but little did he know I held secrets just like him. It was yet another lesson he had taught me—never reveal your full hand and always keep a few cards hidden up your sleeve.

As he casually smoothed back his thick salt-and-pepper hair, his piercing gray eyes narrowed ever so slightly.

He sensed something was up, but he couldn't quite put his finger on it. After all, this was our usual meeting spot, and my request for a meeting wasn't unusual. Nevertheless, he remained vigilant as he settled into his seat across from me.

"Morning, Avra," he greeted in his no-nonsense manner. "What's this about?"

Straight to the point, as always. Vik had little tolerance for beating around the bush, and impatience was a defining aspect of his personality.

I hesitated before speaking, knowing Vik wouldn't like what I said. He scanned our surroundings again, even though I had already done so myself.

But considering who we were and what we were hiding from, being cautious was second nature to us—our time in

Prague with fake identities provided by Vik had been about staying safe.

But now I was done hiding. The fire inside me burned too bright for that. It was time for justice and taking back what was rightfully ours.

And so, without further hesitation, I began the conversation with a punch: "I've found evidence that my parents' deaths were not accidental but a planned assassination."

"This isn't news," Vik replied calmly. "We've suspected this since we came here."

"But now I have proof."

While living in Prague with my sisters and Vik for years, this desire to learn the truth had burned within me. The memories of that night never faded—the chaos, panic, and fear still haunted me to this day.

At fifteen years old, I'd seen through the deception of adults and remembered how our aunt, Theia Cloe, had forced us out of our home that night. She claimed it was for our protection, but something didn't add up. Why hadn't she come with us if she truly wanted us to be safe? How had she known we were in danger? It wasn't until I asked her these questions that she slapped me and told me to do as she said. That was when I knew she was involved and vowed to one day see her downfall.

"What proof?" Vik asked, still maintaining his calm and collected demeanor.

He rarely showed any emotion, always trying to teach us how to keep our vulnerabilities in check.

Suppressing the anger that boiled within me whenever I

thought of Theia Cloe and her use of Vik's methods, I continued with my mission.

"My sources have uncovered that dear Theia Cloe was sleeping with Ozias Xenos." I couldn't help but raise an eyebrow at Vik's barely noticeable reaction, a slight tightening of his lips.

"It's interesting how the man who murdered my mother was also heavily involved in my father's assassination."

"What evidence do you have? Multiple people shot your father in the middle of the city," he reminded me, not arguing but simply stating the facts.

I nodded. "The money trail. It all leads back to Ozias. He orchestrated it all. And my sources have also revealed that others were involved in this plot—those responsible for dividing up my family's territory. Their soldiers carried out the hit on my father."

Vik remained quiet, taking in my words. I knew he had heard every word—he never missed a beat.

After a few moments of contemplation, he leaned forward in his seat and placed his hands firmly on the table. Once again, he scanned our surroundings, asking, "Where did you get this information?"

"From my sources in America," I replied confidently.

I didn't need to remind him that the Vitalis family had cousins worldwide, including in Boston.

Our distant relatives held tight to values of honor and family loyalty, especially regarding Papa, my sisters, and me.

They never accepted the official story surrounding our father's death or our sudden disappearance from Greece.

Over the last ten years, they had discreetly conducted their own investigations, determined to uncover the truth.

In addition, they kept a lock on all things financially tied to the family, making sure to keep it out of the hands of those who'd stolen the Vitalis territory.

When I had reached out to them for help, they welcomed me and my sisters back into the fold with open arms and generously shared all the information they had gathered.

There were no malicious intentions in keeping this from Vik. However, I knew that regaining control of my life meant making my own decisions.

Nothing would stop me from taking my seat as the head of the region and destroying my enemies.

Vik hummed a slight noise, shook his head, picked up the coffee set in front of him, and leaned back in his chair.

As Papa's trusted second for years, Vik was well aware of the inner workings of Papa's empire, including the many Vitalis sources worldwide. He knew that most of them were family in one way or another. He would narrow down those working with me based on the clue I'd given him about Boston.

As he sipped his coffee and contemplated the information I had shared with him, I could see his mind working through the facts. He had undoubtedly considered reaching out to our relatives over the past decade but had prioritized keeping my sisters and me safe above all else.

He sighed heavily and gave me a serious look. "Your plans..." he began.

I lifted my chin, daring him to disagree with me. He

knew my desire to return home and take back what was rightfully ours.

"I worry about them," he confessed. "I am concerned for your safety."

As you've always been. I exhaled and smiled softly. Vik made it his life mission to ensure the safety of my sisters and me. With lectures and lessons about strategizing. Through countless hours of defense and fighting training. And during all the meetings about starting a new financial security system here, away from Greece. Safety was Vik's goal, and I respected him for it.

Nothing would fill the hole in my heart from losing my parents. No one could ever replace my father, but I hoped Vik would always know how much he meant to me and my sisters.

He was a friend, a hero, an uncle, and a surrogate parent when we needed someone to look after us. He wanted to protect me and my sisters. It was his nature, having filled that role for so long, but he was no longer in charge of me in that way. He had to step back from father figure to adviser.

At the time of our parents' deaths, he was only in his late thirties and at the height of his career and wealth. But he willingly gave it all up to protect us. In the blink of an eye, he sacrificed everything to smuggle us out of Greece and create new lives for us with new identities.

Without Vik's bravery and sacrifice, we would not have survived. He truly was our savior, and I hoped he knew how much we appreciated everything he had done for us.

We had escaped to Prague, our lives now shrouded in

secrecy and deceit. It was Vik who orchestrated our disappearance, allowing the world to believe that all four of us had perished during the chaos following Papa's assassination. Thanks to the new identities and lifestyles that Vik meticulously designed, Layana, Calista, and I were able to begin afresh.

But despite his efforts, Vik carried a heavy burden of guilt for not being there when we needed him most. He grieved the loss of our parents, and it pained him to see us struggle without them. Yet, it wasn't his fault. He was our protector and provider.

Vik's lips pressed together in a somber line as he spoke. "You deserve so much better than what you have experienced. Layana and Calista too."

I could sense the weight of his remorse, but I couldn't bring myself to respond. Emotions were not something we openly expressed with each other—it was a survival tactic we'd learned from years of living on the run.

"Have your sisters agreed to your plan?" Vik asked after a moment of silence.

A small smile tugged at the corners of my lips. "Yes. They want justice just as much as I do."

"I have no doubt," he replied in a deep voice.

"We want revenge for it all," I declared firmly, my voice rising slightly with each word. "From my aunt to the man who murdered Mama and everyone involved in Papa's assassination. We will make them pay for destroying our family."

Vik's brows furrowed in concern as he asked, "Are they prepared?"

"They are," I replied confidently. "They understand the sacrifices required to achieve justice. Our days of living in fear and hiding are over."

There was no other choice. We either took action or lived with a cloud of dread over our heads for the rest of our lives. And what kind of existence was that?

Vik nodded, sensing the determination in my words. "Can I assume you plan to do this with or without my approval?"

"I'm not here to ask for permission," I smirked, lifting a challenging brow.

He let out a resigned sigh. "I'll prepare our men to await your orders."

A thrill of anticipation raced through me at his words.

These were the loyalists who never forgot and always believed in honor and duty to the Vitalis family. They were stationed throughout Greece, ready to act on my signal.

Over the years, Vik had kept them close, using them as our eyes and ears in different parts of Greece. When the coup had occurred, they had hidden in plain sight while I disappeared with my sisters. But Vik ensured we always had a small team available to protect us. Over time, he expanded that group into a larger force, but it wasn't enough for what I had planned.

It was time to mobilize.

Vik pulled out his phone and scanned the surroundings until he locked gazes with one of my security guards. A silent conversation passed between them, and I couldn't help but shake my head at Vik's need to protect us constantly.

"I suspected this day would come sooner rather than later," he said in a deadpan tone that brought a smile to my lips. "You were never one to sit idly by once you set your mind on something."

"What have you been doing to prepare?" I asked curiously.

He turned his phone toward me, showing me its screen. "I've been watching properties suitable for purchase in Patras."

I took the device and quickly skimmed over the listing details and images until I found one property in particular that was everything I could hope for—four bedrooms, luxurious, and conveniently located near the city center.

"This is perfect," I said, pointing to it. "Buy it."

"Under your name?" Vik raised a questioning brow, his worry for my plan evident.

I shook my head. "No. I want to make it as difficult as possible for anyone in Patras to learn that the Vitalis sisters are still alive and well."

"This is smart. The element of surprise keeps things in our favor."

The timing was critical.

In a month, my sisters and I would return to the city of our birth. Even if it wasn't to the estate we'd left under the cover of the night, it was on Vitalis territory.

I couldn't wait to see their faces.

Hell hath no fury like the Vitalis sisters seeking their revenge.

Two

E lias

A long, hot shower was all I wanted.

I never tolerated disloyalty. And if it meant covering my hands in blood as I disciplined an idiot who thought he could walk around sharing information not intended for the public, so be it.

The example I set today would make it clear that I tolerated no disrespect from anyone in my organization.

Elimination wasn't my preferred method. However, I needed to soil my hands to clarify my point in cases like this one.

I hadn't expected the time it had taken to delve into the discipline. Then again, allowing the fucker a quicker death wouldn't have the intended impact on others who thought to betray me.

Why the fuck my father had favored that moron, I'd never know. My father's outrage at being deceived amused me. I'd seen it coming but kept quiet, knowing he thought of himself as a pristine judge of character.

Then again, assholes stuck together. And as long as my father *thought* he was the boss around here, the head of the Xenos enterprise and our family, I gave him the illusion of appeasing him when I could and cleaned up his messes.

A traitor was a traitor, after all, and I wasn't called a ruthless killer for nothing.

I passed into the corridor leading to the residential area of the Xenos estate, eyeing the stairs leading to my section of the house.

"Eli? A word," my father called out, forcing me to pause and curl my lip.

Asshole wanted a word after I cleaned up yet another of his messes.

Was he even aware that the majority of his men thought him weak?

To breathe the same air in a room with the asshole was a vile prospect, but that was the role of an obedient only son. As always, I pushed back the loathing, the hatred, the disgust for the man responsible for half of my DNA and turned to stride in the direction of the hallway leading to my father's office.

The stench of blood covering my skin wafted up, adding to my annoyance.

I expected some complaints about my appearance and pungent scent. So if I ruined his expensive, plush carpet, it was his fault.

Facing him was my version of torture. I'd allow my disgusting smell to be his.

One guard outside my father's office inclined his head as I approached and gestured to his pocket, indicating his phone. He was an informant of mine embedded with my father's men, and it seemed he had some information to share.

Age and circumstance had made my father the head of the family, but everyone involved in our sphere understood who really ran things around here.

It wasn't him. Ozias Xenos was *not* the man making this family successful. Due to my blood and sweat, the family rolled in wealth and luxury. Because of my determination and hard work, everyone could live in opulence and with reverence.

Everyone, like the lazy asshole on the other side of that desk.

I entered my father's office and kept my expression blank as he lifted his face toward me. He cared too much about the past and what everyone around him had. He only prioritized the territories he had no control over instead of developing the areas he ran.

Like a lousy leader.

He sat there expectant, dressed as if he were some elderly statesman ready for a night on the town and without a single care in the world. His office was more of a showpiece surrounded by the luxury of expensive art and antiquities. It was a display of his ego, not of his power, as he believed.

His lip curled as he took in my appearance.

"What is it?" I asked, not giving two shits about speaking to him with respect.

This man had long since lost it. The best I could muster was a somewhat civil conversation as I'd have with a soldier who annoyed the shit out of me, but I had to supervise and tolerate.

He grunted and smirked as he sat back in the ornate chair. Swiveling side to side, he sighed and regarded my disheveled appearance. "Rough day?"

"I took care of your misjudgment in character." I shrugged. "It's a messy business. You should try it sometime. Our men like it when the boss gets involved in the work and doesn't lock himself away in the office."

He narrowed his gaze as the barb of truth struck.

"I doubt you want me to stink up your finery. Tell me what you want so I can get out of here," I said, wiping a smear of blood from my brow.

More than likely, this was another discussion about selling tobacco products for our potential alliances with the Italian contacts. Ozias had wanted an exchange arrangement for years but had yet to set it up.

Not until *I* stepped in.

I understood diplomatic maneuvering. Hell, I was more experienced and strategic in my approach to everyone. Maybe once upon a time, he had the touch to charm and negotiate, but he'd lost the edge. Greed compromised one's thinking, and Ozias was all things gluttonous.

I'd figured out how to compromise and still achieve my

goal, specifically the group we dealt with in the northern territories. Showboating had never worked with them. Unfortunately, that was my father's signature antic. Instead, I laid everything out on the table with a clear pair of options: they took it or walked away—all or nothing. The Italians were aware that we had other avenues to move our products. Once they realized my proposals indicated a mutually beneficial process, things fell into place.

Still, Ozias insisted on trying to look like the bigger power, thinking he possessed the influence to exert more expectations on the Italians. If he tried that tactic, he'd never get it.

He stared at me, keeping me in suspense, his fingers steepled together and pressed to his lips. I'd pissed him off, and now he wanted me to stew in my filth and need of a long, hot shower.

"I'm not in the mood for games," I warned him. "Either tell me what you want or—"

"A marriage offer has come to the table."

I went still, pausing to take in his statement.

Marriage?

That was the last thing I expected.

An offer for a bride wasn't unusual. Arranged marriages were common in our world. They linked syndicates, creating alliances and business ties.

For me, an offer of marriage wasn't something I had ever anticipated hearing from Ozias's lips.

I studied Ozias for any signs he was lying or fucking with me and found none.

Who could it be? The only eligible woman he might consider was my last lover, Francesca.

If that was the case, then the answer was no.

She was beautiful, skilled at pleasing me in bed, and came from a family of standing among Ozias's circle, but I'd made it clear from the very beginning that I had no plans to marry her. I'd recognized her clingy and needy nature and set the rules so there was no miscommunication. Our relationship was casual at best, a dalliance over the last year where we enjoyed our time together, nothing more.

Yes, every man would want a gorgeous woman on his arm. But Francesca?

No. Fucking Francesca and marrying her were two very different things.

Besides, the last thing I wanted was to marry anyone or have sex with the same woman over and over again for the rest of my life.

I wasn't a cheater like my father. Marriage meant vows to honor. To marry meant I would only fuck my wife, and I wasn't in any rush to settle like that. I'd managed to avoid marriage for forty years.

Why was the old man pushing it now?

For one obvious fucking reason.

To control me since he hated how everyone knew the truth that I ran the family for him.

"Is that so?" I asked, sarcastic and curious.

I wouldn't show him how intrigued I was by this game he played. Revealing my emotions would be an error with him.

He grinned, slow and sly. "It's Avra Vitalis."

He had to be lying.

I clenched my teeth to avoid betraying a single sign.

Avra Vitalis?

First dropping the bomb of marriage, and now Avra, of all women

I cleared my throat, and I tried to connect the dots. "I thought you eliminated the Vitalis sisters."

My father had never accepted the Vitalis family's power. He'd loathed them so much that he'd stolen it all from them. The Vitalis family had held all the power in Greece. They had been the rulers for many generations—until my father killed them off.

Or, I guess he didn't.

Despite the years that had passed, I remembered everything about the events leading up to that gruesome night, especially Eudora Vitalis's murder, as though it had only happened yesterday.

Ozias had ordered me to "help" him with some work. My job was to start paying my dues for spending years in England finishing my graduate degrees. Fucker told me nothing about his plans outside of taking back what he believed the Vitalises owed to the Xenoses generations ago.

I knew it was bullshit the second those words came out of his mouth. No one owed us anything. Our family history went back over a century, and the Xenoses had started with no land and no prospects. All we had came from a territorial war, unlike the Vitalises, who were gifted their original territory centuries ago by the Greek royal family.

When we arrived at Vitalis's villa outside the city, I questioned Ozias, who told me to follow orders and shut up. As a young idiot, I went inside. He'd set the whole thing up to corner Eudora Vitalis. He knew the remaining Vitalis family wouldn't arrive until morning, and she was alone. Ozias never got over Eudora's rejection of him for Juno. He believed killing her was the prize in his coup on Juno Vitalis.

I would never shake the guilt for my part in her death. I'd tried to stop him, but there was nothing I could do short of taking the bullet for her. He'd killed her right in front of me and told me to grow the fuck up.

And that's what I'd done.

My father's actions had hardened me.

I'd always known he was despicable, but that night changed me.

When I learned of how far he'd stoop, how greedy he'd dare to be, he'd squashed any lingering softness I'd possessed from my deceased mother. He'd forced me to change, to evolve from a young twenty-five-year-old into the heartless killer everyone knew today. Witnessing the effects of Ozias's brutality was a rude awakening, enabling me to accept the life I lived at present.

He stared at me with that knowing smirk I loathed so much. I especially detested how he kept secrets. In other words, I *hated* the asshole.

Now, it looked as if he'd led me—and everyone else—to believe that the sisters had died with their parents.

"Why?" I narrowed my eyes, daring him to mess with me. "Why did you lie?"

He scoffed. "I don't answer to you, *son*."

The fuck you don't.

It wasn't the time to challenge him like that. Soon, but not now.

"Why did you tell everyone that the Vitalis sisters died?"

With a lazy shrug, he swiveled to the other side, his chair squeaking with the move. "I didn't expect them to survive. You remember that night. All that bloodshed."

From your orders.

"I never bothered to look for them. I'd killed all who were loyal to Juno Vitalis."

Apparently, you missed someone, dumbass.

"The sisters have been living in hiding. One of Pello Korba's soldiers heard they had been in Prague all this time. Rumor has it they're back to take what is 'rightfully' theirs." He laughed, easing into a chuckle as he shook his head like it was a stupid joke.

What he said was nothing but the truth. Patras and the territories around it rightfully belonged to the Vitalis family. They had owned them before my father and his three counterparts stole them.

What the fuck are you doing?

I wiped away another smear of sweat and grime from the discipline I'd dished out before coming here. I couldn't understand why Ozias would even consider this marriage offer. He'd be selective. He could resent me for being more powerful within the family, but I was his only son. My choice of a bride would be significant for him, and the fact that he was contemplating Avra Vitalis, the eldest daughter of his former rival, raised suspicions.

I stared at him, trying to pick at his cool indifference and root out what he was scheming. *What are you up to now?*

"Why would you want me to marry her?"

He sighed, scooting his chair back to stand. "The optics would be good."

"What fucking optics?"

He was delusional if he thought he'd fooled anyone. He'd killed his rivals and stolen what was theirs, without remorse or regret.

He pushed to his feet and shoved his hands in his pockets. "I killed her mother, and now my son would be marrying the dead woman's daughter. We've come full circle. It will look like our strength and power brought them out of hiding. That they need us to survive."

How the fuck do you think that if they've been surviving all this time without us?

It hit me then. The truth behind Ozias's statement struck me. If I married Avra, it would legitimize the Xenos claim on the Vitalis territory. Juno Vitalis's will transferred all the deeds and land rights to the Vitalis sisters upon his death. This stately residence, this entire grand estate—all of it. Everything would have gone to the sisters. Now that they were alive and returning, they might want it back.

Still, I found it too convenient. No one offered themselves up to the enemy like this. In our world, the men held the land. The men called the shots.

Ozias may believe this was good fortune falling in his lap.

He seemed ready to assume that Avra's return and offer to marry me would be a twist he could manipulate.

But I wasn't an idiot. I wasn't blind. I understood plots and deceit. I was no stranger to manipulation, and it was good that I knew how to set up and avoid traps.

I see how it is.

I would enjoy being her prey. Then, when she least expected it, I would spring my trap.

"By the way," my father added as he rounded his massive desk.

I tilted my head to the side as he paused before passing me.

"Avra and her sisters will arrive for dinner in thirty minutes. You might want to freshen up for your engagement celebration."

THREE

A vra

I stared out the window, taking in the countryside through the window of the car Vik and I drove in and tried to center myself for the evening again.

My plan was in motion, and there was no turning back.

Returning to Greece and moving my sisters into the house Vik had found took a lot of maneuvering and strategy. Throughout the move, I tried my best to remain numb to the entire ordeal, to the fact that we were no longer going to pretend that we'd died fifteen years ago.

The hiding was all over.

Except, the emotionless façade I had learned to wear so well seemed so fragile tonight. Tonight, Vik and I rode to the estate where my sisters and I had last seen our parents alive. As we drove closer to the massive house, the grief I rarely, if ever, allowed to surface demanded release.

Just looking out the window hurt my soul. There were so many familiar landscape features and nearby areas filled with memories.

No. I couldn't allow myself to fall apart. This wasn't the time for unexpected remembrances to flare up, but to plan, to attack, to...

Be calm. Stay levelheaded. You can do this.

If only my nerves understood the objective and settled down.

No matter what, I refused to allow fear, apprehension, or worry to win. And I'd be damned if I let anyone detect a break in my armor.

Not the driver. Not Vik. Not anyone.

Vik had taught me the fine arts of schooling my features and perfecting a mask of indifference. Now, it was time to apply those lessons.

As Calista liked to call it, my game face would remain unshakeable. I would never let Ozias see a crack in my façade. Of all people, he would only get the tough shell of the woman I had to become because of him. It was all he deserved.

This was for my family. For my sisters' future. For my parents' deaths. For the Vitalis legacy of generations lost. The moment to strike back was here, and I would not entertain the possibility of messing up.

Ozias Xenos had accepted the marriage offer through Vik.

Now, it was time to step into the actual battle and enter the lion's den—my former home.

A motorcade of a few of our loyal soldiers surrounded our vehicle, giving the impression that I wasn't left unprotected. However, the majority of our force would remain hidden throughout the city.

The less others knew of the Vitalis women's strength, the better. It was better to allow all to underestimate us. I wanted them to think we were weak, to believe they had easy targets to attack.

I couldn't wait to see their reactions when the Vitalis loyalists went to every part of the area to take back everything stolen from them.

"You can do this," Vik whispered once we exited the car onto the land that had once borne the name Vitalis.

I remained in place for a moment to take in everything and study, noticing all the familiar features and the changes and new additions. It burned a scalding fire on my heart to see my family home inhabited by the enemy, but it hardly resembled the elegant residence I'd once loved. Ozias had ruined it by being here and renovating it with a hideous, modernistic approach full of excess. The history, the old culture, and simplicity seemed faded and barely visible.

It stung just seeing it.

"You can—"

"I know," I snapped quietly.

Vik only wanted to encourage me, but it was unnecessary. I *knew* I could handle this. It would be hard to return *here*, but I damn well would. Seeking the ultimate revenge had been my motivation to live for so long, and I wouldn't back down or crumble now.

He nodded, smiling a bit at the snark in my reply. He knew me so well that he'd be right to guess I was bitchy because my hesitation irked me. Without another word, he offered me his arm and led me inside.

A servant opened the door and gestured for us to enter. I remained at Vik's side as we passed through the beautiful foyer, now overstuffed with gaudy ornamentation. Footsteps sounded from the left, and I braced myself for the moment to face my enemy.

I'd seen photos of Ozias Xenos. My father had never let us girls get involved with the family business before his murder, so this was my first face-to-face interaction with the bastard himself.

Turning slowly, keeping my face blank and not scowling, I met the self-satisfied gaze of the man who'd ruined my family. This tall man held his head high, looking down his nose at me with the air of a gentleman he could never be.

"Welcome," he greeted with the arrogant comfort of being in charge.

I allowed my gaze to bore into his, silently wishing him dead. Staring into the soul of evil itself, without effort, I envisioned all the ways I could take his life.

I loathed his health and vibrancy, something Papa would never enjoy.

That tall bronze statue on that shelf behind the bastard

caught my attention. It looked perfect. I could smash his head with the hard figure. Over and over until the muscles in my arms burned and blood splattered the wall.

Or perhaps I could grab his silky black tie, wrap it around his neck, and then squeeze and pull until his face turned red and he clawed at my grip for air. Holding on tight, I'd strangle him until he dropped limp to the marble floor.

Or the knife nestled at the small of my back. It was a slim, small blade, but I could greedily make do with it, plunging it into his chest with fierce punches until his heart ceased to beat.

Or—

Vik patted the hand still lying over his arm. Then again, harder. He jarred me from my fierce daydreams of death, reminding me to stay in the present as though he knew what I was thinking.

Shit.

I'd allowed my serene guise to slip.

Immediately, I gave a half-hearted, closed-lipped smile as Ozias Xenos welcomed me into *his* home.

His. *The fuck it is.* This place belonged to my family. It wasn't his to have, nor was it his to claim.

After the expected greetings, Ozias grinned at me and asked Vik, "What about the sisters?" He glanced past us, making it clear that his invitation was an order for my sisters and me to follow.

"They couldn't make it." I kept my reply simple and direct.

Ozias furrowed his brow, losing that cool, charming look. Then he raised his brows in a silent question.

I didn't elaborate. He didn't deserve an explanation for my sisters' whereabouts.

"They are not coming to dinner?"

I shook my head. "They couldn't make it."

My repeated reply had him scoffing. His annoyance was my triumph, and I intended to ride the satisfying high of irritating him for as long as I could.

I couldn't linger in the victory for long. As I realized I was in a stare-off with this asshole, I felt a telltale sensation on the back of my neck. A sixth-sense awareness that never failed, always alerting me to someone watching me. It was a burn, a gnawing tingle I couldn't ignore.

As I lifted my gaze and glanced to the side, I found piercing dark eyes watching my interaction with Ozias.

He was tall and handsome, with a few features similar to the man before me, but he carried an edge that screamed he was the dangerous one.

Elias. My fiancé. My future husband.

The son of the bastard who'd murdered my mother.

I stood straighter, knowing the second-hardest task of the night was upon me. I stared back at him, unflinching as he pushed off the wall from where he'd positioned himself in the corner of the room, sizing me up.

He approached with sure, steady steps. Something about the way he looked at me made my pulse jump and things deep inside me awaken.

The closer he came, the more I struggled to remember that he had a purpose—he was a means to an end.

Long legs quickly covered the distance between us. Each step he took pulled at the fabric covering his thick, firm, muscled legs. That suit fit him without a flaw, accentuating the sculpted planes of his chest and the sturdy strength of his muscular arms. Slow and steady, he stalked toward me like a predator homing in on his prey.

Prey? I would be no such conquest.

I couldn't forget this was my enemy. Marrying him would get me in a position to destroy the asshole who'd created him.

But as he loomed before me, just tall enough that I had to tip my face up to meet his eyes, I realized he was already complicating what I intended him to be.

I found him more than attractive.

What the ever-loving fuck?

Gazing into his deep brown eyes, I resisted this growing fascination that sparked and sizzled. He remained unsmiling and neutral, almost bored, as he looked me over. Everywhere he dragged his lazy stare felt like a tangible caress.

As his attention lingered on my lips, something deep, warm, unwanted, and visceral awoke.

I fought to stay unaffected.

My reputation was critical to being calm and composed. I wouldn't forget this, and I couldn't ignore it.

But my heart raced, and a stupid part of me enjoyed being the object of his focus.

Of the idea that he could *want* to conquer me with that dark, predatory sensuality he emitted.

The corner of his lips twitched, almost like a smirk. He wanted me to react. This was all a game to him.

Fuck you, asshole.

Avra, you know better.

He was the enemy, nothing more. And damn him to hell if he thought he could incite something like desire to course through me.

This was what I deserved for going without sex for extended periods of time. Men like Elias Ozias could push past my barriers and fuck with me.

"Evening." I kept my tone cold, icy, and formal.

"Evening," he replied without the stiffness I'd shown. "I hope your trip was pleasant."

Asshole. I hadn't taken a *trip.*

I bit my lip. "Most pleasant."

"Find the house okay?" he asked, again suggesting he might be bored.

Of course, I knew how to find this address. I used to live here!

"Certainly," I replied. I'd be calm if it killed me.

Elias Xenos wouldn't get a rise out of me, not like this.

I hoped he wouldn't notice the slight clench in my jaw, but as he watched me intensely, studying me, I wasn't sure if he was acting this indifferent.

Was he fighting a *smile?*

This man made no sense.

I shifted my attention to Vik and Ozias as they spoke

about the future of our families and fought the urge to glance back at Elias.

I knew he watched me, taking in everything about me. I felt the weight of his interest. Was he as confused by me as I was by him?

I gave in, peeking at him as we moved to the dining room. His eyes locked on my lips again. He jerked, looking away with a muttered curse, and I realized this attraction between us might be mutual. He was quicker to hide it.

The next thirty minutes were a charade of stilted small talk and discussions, with Ozias taking center stage. Elias and I spoke on and off with quick banter given in cool, indifferent tones during the horrendous half hour but allowed his father to remain in charge.

What I hadn't anticipated was actually enjoying his company.

Dammit. The chance of a connection like this pissed me off even more.

First, I found him attractive, and now I enjoyed his company.

My annoyance with my situation grew as soon as we were seated in the dining room. Ozias had ruined my family home. He had renovated and left his mark on the room, transforming it into a garish mix of gold and gray—an overwhelming display of wealth devoid of style. All the art and antiques that had once been there were gone, replaced entirely by steel and glass.

By the time the meal was over, my exhaustion had surpassed anything I'd experienced after all the work involved in moving my family from another country. Ozias dominated nearly every conversation, addressing Vik almost exclusively.

Men ran things in the syndicate world. I knew this. I had lived in it my entire life.

But for them to plan the wedding as if my opinion were of no consequence.

I tried to tune it out. To stay cool. To remain blank. To—

I gritted my teeth, catching myself glancing at Elias again. To stop looking at him.

He did the same, letting his father take charge of the conversation.

I resisted a scowl as I met Elias's intense and curious gaze while Ozias told Vik what he wanted to happen with the wedding.

Was my future husband amused? Did he enjoy seeing me sit here like an angry, silent *thing*? I held back a growl, furious at the thought that he might view me as a toy, as if I were here for his entertainment.

"A month?" Vik asked in reply to Ozias's expectations for the wedding date.

My friend looked at me, brows raised, and I nodded. It hardly mattered when it happened, just that it would.

"The venue will be at a Greek Orthodox church," Ozias continued.

I lost my fight with a huff, laughing once. "Well, that should work out well, considering I'm Greek Orthodox."

Ozias dropped his fork with a clatter, agitated as he narrowed his eyes at me. The bright gold on his hand caught my attention with the movement. His thick, squat ring on his pinky reflected the chandelier's lights, momentarily distracting me and delaying my response with the full extent of my wrath.

"Don't wait for me to excuse myself." *I'll speak up as much as I want.* "Seeing as it's my wedding, it might be important to involve the bride." I glanced at Elias, who, at that moment, refused to look up from his food. "Or the couple." Damn, it felt weird to say that out loud. A *couple.* With him.

"I understand you might be lacking education," Ozias lectured. "Your father hasn't been around to teach you these things. But women don't speak in a men's discussion." He wagged his finger at me like I was a child, taunting me to reach over and break it.

"My father *hasn't* been around," I agreed as I tossed my napkin to the table, ready to unleash my fury. "But—"

"But *I* have been," Vik cut in, warning me not to let my temper get to me. "And I've instructed her to speak up when necessary."

Ozias grunted and shook his head. "Funny, isn't it? That you reappeared after all this time. We all believed you were dead."

Vik shrugged, holding his hands out as though to say *think again.*

I clamped my lips shut. Vik's reminder to keep a lid on my temper helped me to rein it in. Arguing with Ozias wouldn't serve justice. This wasn't the endgame. If he wanted to feel like a king and be in control, so be it. He would get what he deserved.

All the while, I felt Elias's eyes on me. He didn't speak up. He observed me as though he wanted to find my tells and discover a trick.

"It doesn't matter. This will be my wedding, and I will have a say," I said, steering the topic away from my father.

"The hell you will. If you become a Xenos, you will do things *my* way."

"Or else?" I taunted. "Just what is the *Xenos* way?"

Ozias's nostrils flared as he seethed, staring daggers at me.

"How about a stroll outside?" Elias stood so fast, dropping his utensils on the table, that I barely had a chance to prepare for his suggestion. "Let's get some fresh air."

It wasn't an offer but a firm order. I narrowed my eyes at the gorgeous man as he held his hand out. Ignoring it, I pushed my chair back and stood alone, gritting my teeth once I gave Vik and Ozias my back.

The second I was outside, I closed my eyes at how they'd butchered the gardens and changed it all. It was hideous, nothing like the natural grounds Mama used to love so much.

Can I even do this? Live here where so many memories linger? Can I live under a roof with that horrible man? Playing charades had never seemed so hard.

I reacted to the touch of Elias's hand on the small of my back, right near the hilt of the blade I wore there.

Instead of commenting, he trailed his fingers upward, warming my skin, and then said, "We won't live with him."

I blinked once, surprised by how Elias could have read

my mind about his father and ignored the fact that I carried a weapon into his house.

This man was dangerous, and I couldn't let my guard down.

He gestured, directing me away from the doors.

Once we had some distance from the house, he crossed his arms and, point-blank, asked, "Why are you offering yourself up to the big bad wolf as a sacrificial lamb in marriage?"

"You?" I scoffed. "Big bad wolf? Please."

He lowered his arms and stepped closer, glowering at me. "Answer me."

I swallowed but didn't allow any other sign of awareness. Not just loathing or sarcasm, but how much Elias's clean, spicy scent overwhelmed me this close. "I want my children to have my legacy." It wasn't a lie. I wouldn't have my family name, but I'd have this place. I only had to marry him for his name's sake, giving me some power back in the process. I'd have the territory, which was a step forward in the plan for revenge and justice.

He leaned in, taunting me with his scent and the warmth radiating from his rugged body. With a seductive whisper that sent goosebumps along my shoulder and arm, he pushed back. "I think you're a wolf hiding in sheep's clothing."

Shit.

"Why are you questioning me?" I wouldn't reply and deny his guess.

"Why are you insulting me, insisting you have no ulterior motive?"

"Who said I do?" I shot back.

"I'm not blind. Nor am I stupid."

"You're—" I slammed my lips shut, aware with stark clarity how close I'd leaned in and how frustrated he seemed.

We both breathed heavily and quickly, stirred up from more than one disagreement. Sizzling between us was nothing but sexual tension, torrid and stubborn. It was a distraction I would not acknowledge to him.

I stepped back, needing a chance to breathe without his scent muddying my mind.

"I know you're up to something."

"You don't *know* me."

"I will. And I already can tell you're scheming. I plan to find out what."

I tipped my chin up, pursed my lips, and lifted a brow. His eyes darkened, and for a flash, I saw pure, unadulterated lust staring at me.

"Sometimes," he said, leaning closer once more before passing me to return to the house, "the most dangerous creatures are the beautiful ones."

Four

After dinner, Vik and I left the house in the car our driver had left behind. As soon as we reached the main road outside the estate, I took a long, deep breath.

"That fucking bastard." Vik pounded his hand on the steering wheel.

He wasn't inclined to show emotions, but seeing the place ruined and transformed like that, with Ozias lording his control over my family's home, had affected even him.

I nodded, gazing out the window momentarily to collect my composure. Now that I was out of Elias's presence and free of Ozias's, I wanted to decompress. To simmer down from being on edge.

But there was no time for it.

"Are you all right?"

I shot him a side-eye as he drove.

"I want to make sure you're confident in your plan."

"What, did you think seeing him would scare me off?" I shifted in my seat and reached under my dress to unclasp the holder for my blade, pulling it free from my waist before tucking it into a compartment at my feet.

Vik shook his head. "No, but..."

"But nothing. It's too late, even if I want to change my mind. We've revealed ourselves. We're here. We're back." I swallowed hard. "And we're targets again."

"What about him, though? Elias?"

I arched one brow, trying to figure out his concerns.

"I noticed the tension between you."

I opened my mouth to remind Vik that Elias had to view me as the enemy as much as I did him, but I clamped my lips shut, trapping my retort in my mouth. I couldn't blame our family rivalry for *all* the tension that had sparked in the air.

Elias wasn't anything I anticipated. It was disconcerting how this energy pulsed between us. And then there was how he looked at me when he walked me to the car, possessive and territorial.

It made no sense.

No, what made no sense was that I had no problem with it.

Then, while we were in the garden, his dominance and no-nonsense tone made me feel alive and charged. I'd argued with him.

The last thing I expected was this sudden awareness, this unexplainable need to be near him. Something about him made me want to push every one of his buttons, to challenge him, and see how he handled someone who took none of his shit.

The physical attraction to Elias Xenos was one thing. Still, the temptation of learning about the beast I saw lurking in those eyes was another.

"I did some digging on him," Vik said, snapping me from my thoughts.

"On Ozias?" *Obviously.*

"Elias."

That was news to me. "I thought we already had everything possible on the Xenos family."

"There is always more to find out. Once word of your marriage offer spread, people talked."

"And? What did you find?"

I needed to go into this marriage with all the information possible. I couldn't go in unprepared if he could unsettle me with one evening.

"Elias is extremely private."

Great. Then he can keep to himself and not bother me.

"He doesn't like his father."

Elias's comment about not living with Ozias at that house had helped me figure this out.

"He also has a lover who won't like that he's off the market. So you should be ready for that as well."

I smirked. "For what? A scorned lover? I'm not some weak woman who can't stand my ground with others."

"I'd think not. Get prepared for the next part of tonight's adventure." He turned the car, heading away from the house I shared with him and my sisters for now.

I'd be moving again in a month. Tonight, though, I had another stop to make.

I nodded. "I wonder if she'll remember me."

Vik and I had made the preparations for this crucial step in my grand plan, but now that the moment was here, I wondered if I could pull off this next part. Offering myself as a "sacrificial lamb in marriage" had been easy. Facing Ozias and Elias at dinner was difficult. But this?

"She'll remember as soon as she gets a good look at you."

I licked my lips, envisioning the last time I saw my aunt. She'd pushed me through the tunnels under the estate, urgent and desperate for me to flee without giving me a chance to return to my mother's lifeless body and tell her goodbye. I was the one who'd found her there on the ground.

Theia Cloe insisted vehemently that I take my sisters and leave. She practically pushed Laya and Cali into the stairwell. I felt obligated to follow them, aware of the darkness surrounding us and that I was their only support.

I clenched my fist as the memory returned in full force. Cali had only been five at the time, crying as she clutched me tight. I'd held her as we hurried through the tunnels, pushed to run from the sheer terror Theia Cloe instilled in us. Cali had reached her hand back as I carried her away, and I would never forget her pleas and tears, sobbing for our parents.

Reminded of that hellish night, I knew I was ready. I was more than ready.

"Here." Vik handed me a duffel bag, and I took it without question.

I crawled into the back of the car and changed into the clothes we'd set aside in there. Layering a shirt over my dress, then pants beneath it, I pulled off an entirely new outfit without revealing anything indecent. I'd learned the trick under Vik's training when he'd coached all three of us girls on how to manage a swift disguise on the go, should we ever need it.

As I shifted in my seat, ensuring everything fit, Vik pulled up to the curb a few streets from Theia Cloe's home.

"For Juno and Eudora," Vik said.

I nodded at him once, then exited the car without giving him any other response.

I needed to go. I had to do this. Now that I was here, hidden in street clothes to disguise my identity from any street cameras, I flipped the hood of my jacket up and walked to her door.

I could have had my men do this. Letting them handle it would have kept my hands clean.

Vik had volunteered to handle the situation.

Laya had even offered to take care of this step.

Still, it had to be me.

It was my plan and my responsibility to do it.

This was about justice, looking her in the face and making her understand the depth of her betrayal of the family.

A leader never told others to complete their dirty work.

As the eldest sister, the mastermind behind this plan for revenge, I had no choice but to do so.

I am the Vitalis. I will not fail the family.

The door opened, and at first, Theia Cloe kept the wood panel cracked. She peered at me, narrowing her eyes in suspicion. "I'm not interested. No solicitors."

Before she could shut the door, I stuck my foot forward and flipped my hood back.

She squinted more, then opened her eyes wider in recognition.

"Eudora..." She gasped. "Avra?"

Blinking rapidly, she lowered her guard. I'd surprised her, all right. Her mouth dropped open as she gawked at me with wide-open eyes.

"You look just like your mother." She'd uttered it as a whisper of awe, of stunned shock, and so thrown off by my appearance. She released the door.

It swung open, and I waited for no invitation, striding right in. I slowed only to shut the door behind me.

"I—I just can't believe it. You've grown. You— My goodness, Avra. Look at you."

I stood back, hands on my hips, as she stared. "And look at you. Still, the traitorous bitch who helped kill my parents."

"What?" She snapped her brows together and scowled immediately.

But I saw it. I caught that fleeting, instant sweep of fear in her eyes.

"You were involved with Papa's and Mama's deaths." I wasn't there to ask.

I had no doubt that she had helped Ozias ruin my family. My sources in America had no incentive to lie, and they'd spent years seeking evidence to back up this accusation.

Tonight was nothing more than a confrontation—a final one, long past due.

"You're insane." She shook her head. "I never...I would never—"

"No?" I didn't budge, glaring at her without a break, waiting for her to fess up.

"No! I wouldn't have ever gotten involved with something like that."

"I don't believe you."

She huffed, shaking her head at me as she walked around the sofa, placing more distance between us. That was all she'd wanted back then. She'd ordered me to go with my sisters. Reinstating a buffer between us now would do her no good. I was onto her, and I refused to be swayed by her pleas.

Taking in the details of her parlor room, I homed in on the artwork hung on the walls. It was in the same bold and modern style as what Ozias had in his home. A few pieces bore the signatures of the same artist. And then there were the liquor snifters with the same symbols etched on them as those my enemy had.

Even the scents that lingered in the air stank of his cologne.

The crest on her necklace cemented that my aunt continued to lie as she protested my accusation and rambled about how she'd never turn her back on her sister.

As she spoke louder, more passionately, to con me into

considering her lies of innocence, the pendant slipped from its spot beneath the neckline of her shirt. Gaudy gold slid free, reflecting in the light. It was the same design Ozias had on that fat ring. He wore it on the pinky of his right hand. I'd just seen it at dinner. And spotting the same fucking thing on my aunt was all the proof I ever could have needed to see with my eyes.

Rage filled me. A sweeping wave of fury crested through me, and I strained to keep calm and not reveal how close to lashing out I was.

"And I— I..." Theia Cloe faltered, realizing that I stared at the necklace. She lifted her fingers to her neckline, touched the shiny metal, and tucked it beneath her shirt again. "You're not thinking clearly," she warned, likely picking up on how I'd pieced things together.

Crystal clear. "Do your children know that you cheated on their father with another man?"

"I didn't!"

I was on a roll. "Did you have their father killed like you did mine?"

She slashed her hand through the air. "No! I'm telling you, no—"

"Because I doubt very much that Theios Stenos died of a heart attack."

She pressed her lips together so tightly that her chin trembled. Then she wagged a finger at me like I was a naughty child displeasing her, just like her lover had done earlier. The mimicry gave me the urge to snarl.

"I won't have you telling anyone these lies."

I laughed. "The truth, you mean. Everyone knows you weren't faithful. It was an open secret."

Theia Cloe shook her head as she crossed the room. I didn't follow her. I could let her have this last-minute need for distance. It wouldn't save her. I became more alert as she moved toward the bar, as though she wanted to refill her glass and pour a drink.

She kept her gun near the decanters. She always had. My cousins had mentioned this long ago. I'd been gone for fifteen years, but I remembered regardless. It seemed Theia Cloe hadn't changed her habits.

As she hurried toward the bar, I watched her with different eyes. She was no longer the bitter aunt I could never quite feel close to. She was no longer the relative who was always ready to criticize her sister or scoff at my father.

She wasn't family.

Not to me.

All I saw was her deception. Her cruelty. Her pathetic hopelessness as she arranged to eradicate my mother and father.

Reaching around my waist, I grabbed the weapon I'd tucked into the back of my waistband as Vik drove. The hooded jacket hid it from any eyes on the street.

My blade wasn't necessary for the task ahead.

As I waited for my aunt to turn around and face me, it was up and out in the open, ready for use.

The second Theia Cloe spun and pointed her gun, I shot her between the eyes, one single shot. All the training and practice under Vik's tutelage had some benefits.

Theia Cloe's wasn't the first life I'd taken, but the initial one in my journey for revenge.

I stood there, enjoying her pain and anguish as she stumbled and then slumped to the floor. A wave of relief and peace settled over me right before I gave her the last words I'd rehearsed in my mind for years.

"This is for your betrayal. You've paid your debt to the Vitalis family. May God show you the mercy you refused to give your sister."

FIVE

E lias

Two days after I saw Avra at dinner, I strode out of the house, ready to handle a situation with one of our men. It was the last thing I wanted to deal with, considering the shitty night's rest I had gotten.

For two days, I'd struggled to stop thinking about Avra. I wasn't obsessed, far from it. A pair of nice tits and a fine ass were nothing to get crazy about. I had my pick of gorgeous women.

Then why couldn't I get Avra Vitalis out of my mind?

She'd even crept into my dreams last night. How the fuck had I allowed that to happen?

She was beautiful. That was an undeniable truth—Avra

was stunning, especially when angry. More than once, I envisioned how she'd looked the night we first met. So collected and calm, her chin tipped up as my father tried to dismiss her.

Then there was how her long brown hair cascaded over her shoulders as she verbally sparred with me outside. She wanted to make it clear she wasn't weak. I understood that from the moment I laid eyes on her. However, my focus returned over and over to her plump lips, firm and begging to be kissed.

On paper, she was an ideal one to call my wife, well pedigreed and beautiful. Only a fool would reject the offer of marriage to her. But that was what she wanted everyone to see.

That was more than the truth when she said I didn't know her. Soon, I'd know everything about her and her secrets. I planned to learn what she hid under that façade of the strong, cold, unbendable woman.

I'd glimpsed a moment of her fire as she held her own on the patio. I couldn't wait to spar with her. She waved a red flag to a feral bull, and I wanted to coax out all the passion or anger she locked up inside her.

Maybe I was a sadistic bastard. Then again, my only distractions came in the form of work. This would be a pleasant change to the mundanity of my life.

I gritted my teeth, thinking of what I needed to do today for that aspect of my world. An hour earlier, I'd received information that one of our people had hit a woman on the street, with numerous witnesses. I had my men grab and hold him for me to deal with. This dumbass represented the Xenos name. His behavior reflected on us. To keep a territory, those who lived in it needed to respect us and believe we protected them. We protected the weak, not abused them.

Of course, the fucker worked for Ozias. His people were the ones causing the problems. How many lessons would I need to teach before they learned what I would and wouldn't tolerate?

Particularly with this grievance. I was a hard man. I killed and beat plenty. But striking a woman would sign a fucker's death warrant.

Even Ozias knew better than to smack any woman around. And he'd learned that lesson the hard way when I caught him raising his fist at my mother. I was only fourteen then, but I nearly matched his size, rivaling him in strength. The second I saw him strike my mother, I punched him directly in the nose. Our guards had rushed forward but stayed uncertain of what to do, considering the situation.

If my mother hadn't pleaded for me to stop, I would have punched him over and over until I broke more of his bones. He must have seen something in my eyes that day. Maybe it was the lethal killer I would become, but from that day, he and all those who worked for the Xenos family knew my stance on this wrongdoing. As far as I was concerned, only useless and insecure men hit those who were physically weaker than they were.

"Where is he?" I asked a soldier outside the holding area of the Xenos compound.

"In the cell on the end. He ran as soon as he heard we were looking for him."

Walking into the cell, I paused and then shook my head. "Marcos, what the hell have you done?"

This made absolutely no sense. Marcos was a loyal member of the family's operation. His entire family worked for the Xenos enterprise.

"Explain," I ordered the soldiers, keeping him there. "He has five daughters. This is the last thing he would do."

"Several witnesses corroborated that it was him," one replied.

"There's more to this incident. What are you leaving out?"

"If I may add, sir," the other soldier said, "his behavior hasn't been very normal lately."

I stared at Marcos as he hung his head, not even looking at me. "How so?"

The soldier continued. "After his wife died in the territory hit last year, he lost control. His behavior has been erratic, and our supervisor thinks he's been struggling with grief. Lashing out and slipping up."

I sighed, looking back at the defeated man who couldn't find the courage to face me.

I understood grieving the loss of a loved one, but losing control? Over a woman?

Then again, the one man I respected, Pappous Nikko, once told me real men treasured and protected their wives. Without them, a family cannot continue.

I approached Marcos, hurling him up to look directly into his eyes. "Tell me what happened."

He hung his head. "I shouldn't have hit Anna."

I punched him just for the sheer fact that he'd abused someone weaker than him. His blood splattered onto my shirt, making me shake my head. I had to stop wearing new clothes when I came here.

"Let's not state the obvious. What led up to the incident?"

"The neighbors caught her giving my girls alcohol. All are under thirteen. I confronted her, and she laughed at me, saying I let my wife die, and this is what happens when other people have to raise my girls for me."

I felt rage for him.

I knew the background of how he'd lost his wife. He was working for Ozias outside of town when the hit occurred. It was during school pickup. She'd lost her life in the crossfire between our men and a rival family.

I pushed Marcos onto a nearby chair.

"Bring Anna in. We need to have a chat with her."

Marcos's head snapped up. "Don't punish her. She's a young girl, too. Only nineteen. I was wrong for slapping her. She lost her mother too, and is lashing out."

What the ever-loving fuck?

"That isn't an excuse for her behavior. I will have a chat with her and make it clear to get her act in order, that is all."

Marcos nodded, and a tear slipped down his cheek. "She's right, I didn't protect her."

"You are not responsible for this. If anything, Ozias and I are. You were out on orders from us."

He nodded, not saying anything more.

Was this what happened when a man lost his wife? I had never seen Ozias this way when my mother died, but then again, he never cared for her a single ounce.

How would I react if I were to lose Avra—

What the hell? We weren't even married yet, and here I was, projecting and thinking of what could happen if she died before me.

We lived a vicious, violent life. We protected our spouses and children by staying ahead of rivals, but there were occasions when we lost loved ones and suffered. Would Avra grieve me? Or would she scheme and plot to replace me with another?

For fuck's sake. Thinking of what-ifs like a lovesick puppy was ridiculous. I hadn't even married Avra yet.

But I couldn't escape the thoughts. Was it the permanence of it all?

Marriage.

Avra would be my *wife*, not just another woman to warm my bed.

Christ. In a matter of weeks, I planned to tie the rest of my life to another.

If I were to marry Avra and lose her too soon—

I'd be fucked in the head too. Husbands and wives were to grow old together, not die in their youth.

I studied Marcos. There wasn't any way I could kill the sad fuck for this mistake.

Giving leeway wasn't an option either. One lousy mistake could bring down the entire empire.

I wasn't a saint or anything close. He'd get a good beating for this. He'd shamed the Xenos name in public. I would instill a hard-earned lesson by the end of his discipline. He lived today because I wasn't a complete spawn from hell.

My men would make sure he cleaned up his act. If he didn't, he knew what would happen.

"The *only* reason I'm sparing your life this time is because your wife just died. Because you have innocent daughters waiting for you at home. But"—I leaned over him, gripped his bloody chin, and raised his face until he met my gaze—"you are never to put your hands on a woman again. I don't care what they say or do. Shoot them before you touch them. Is that clear?"

He nodded, trembling with the effort to remain standing.

I released him, confident he understood there were no second chances.

"You shamed the Xenos name, and that requires restitution. Decide who administers your punishment. Leonos or me?"

My head lieutenant and I used different methods for discipline. It would hurt either way.

A beating was a small penance for Marcos, considering who I was. Our world worked based on power and reputation. I wielded a considerable amount, and allowing Marcos to live wasn't something I did.

"You," Marcos said, his voice sure and eyes direct.

Thirty minutes later, I walked down the halls of the facility to my car, tired and wondering if I was too hard on Marcos. Logically, I knew I hadn't been. I'd lose control of the territory by giving him too much mercy.

But then I thought again about how I might react if I were in Marcos's place. I definitely wouldn't give anyone like Anna a second chance. Her death would come fast and clean, and I'd make it clear never to mess with my children or the memory of my wife.

Fuck. What was wrong with me? All this wife and child shit was ridiculous.

I needed a shower and a stiff drink.

Running a frustrated hand through my hair, I stalked to my car and opened the door. I barely sat inside when a series of texts appeared on my phone.

"What now?" I muttered to myself.

I unlocked the screen to read the messages.

Ozias: Get to the estate. We have a crisis.

Ozias: Stop ignoring me. When I send a message, I expect an immediate response.

Ozias: It is life and death.

Of course, it was. Everything from a broken chair to an actual stabbing was life and death.

Eli: On my way.

It was better to keep it simple than to engage in a back-and-forth with no functional outcome.

I looked down at myself. Blood splatters covered my shirt, my knuckles stung from the activities with Marcos, and sweat drenched my body.

Exhausted, annoyed, and aggravated were too mild of words for how I felt. However, none of it mattered. I'd play the dutiful son for now, then it would all crumble at Ozias's feet.

When I arrived at the estate my father had stolen for his own, I thought of Avra, wondering how she had felt when she saw the house after fifteen years. I knew how I'd feel.

Pissed as fucking hell. The renovations alone would have enraged me.

I opposed it, preferring the traditional structure and its centuries-old history. However, Ozias wanted to erase as much of Juno Vitalis as possible, so he'd added his own touch to things.

If only a call hadn't delayed me, I would have loved to have seen her initial meeting with Ozias. I could imagine the fire in Avra's eyes and the hate burning there when she locked gazes with him. Luckily, I'd arrived on time to see everything afterward.

Her calm and collected manner made it seem as if she was unapproachable and remote. But she was far from it. I couldn't wait to put cracks in that barrier around her.

Fuck. I ground my teeth as I strode through the house. I had to stop thinking about her. We barely knew each other.

Why the hell were my thoughts constantly going to her?

When I reached my father's office, I found him pacing and muttering. He shook his head right before he gripped the back of his neck tightly. The redness on his face and puffy eyes made it appear like he'd cried.

That was impossible. No matter how mad or upset he became, I'd never seen him cry.

The man was a selfish, arrogant bastard, and seeing him so unhappy and upset was disconcerting.

"What's wrong?" I asked.

He lifted his head, his eyes red-rimmed, and utter devastation etched all over his face.

"Cloe is dead. Murdered. Shot in her own home." His news came in a rush of stilted and broken statements, like he couldn't bear to elaborate on the awful details.

He walked over to his couch and dropped unceremoniously onto it as if he were a broken man.

Well, this was a series of firsts.

Ozias avoided showing weakness at all costs. He would rather die than admit a flaw or vulnerability.

But Cloe, it seemed, could do it.

For most of my life, I knew her as the preferred mistress. He showered her with gifts and chose her as his companion for extended travel, even over my mother, while she was alive.

Affairs were the norm in our world. Mistresses were an expectation, not an oddity or scandal.

From my teen years, I knew about Ozias's relationship with Cloe. I despised her for the pain she caused my mother. Still, I knew expressing my opinion to Ozias wouldn't have made any difference. In fact, it would have caused problems for my mother, so I kept my mouth shut.

Now, seeing him so ragged and torn about the news of Cloe's death, I realized he'd actually cared for her. In the twenty years they'd slept together on and off, my father had never acknowledged her in public.

At first, I thought it was because they both had been married for part of that time, and he respected the need to keep quiet. However, following my mother's and her husband's deaths, my father never labeled her as his girlfriend. Perhaps he was too cautious that such a designation could lend her power over him.

"Are you okay?" I asked. I didn't care. It felt good to see him suffer for a change. But the obligation to inquire was there.

"No. No, I'm not fucking *okay*," Ozias yelled as he resumed his pacing. "I swear I will find whoever was responsible. Until the day I die, I will look. I vow to bring her killer to justice."

I stood there, silent and shocked by the vehemence behind his words. It wasn't so much his vow to avenge as to do it for a lover and not for something associated with the family.

In my entire life, I'd never seen Ozias this emotional or distraught. He barely gave a shit when Mama had learned about her cancer. He had never shed a single goddamn tear when she died.

Nothing.

The fucker loved Cloe. He'd cared about something or someone other than himself for once in his life.

Go figure.

His heart wasn't black and dead.

Knowing I couldn't do anything for this situation, I left

him to stew and brood. Giving him any condolence attempt would be a waste with the feral state he'd waded into.

As I headed toward my suite to wash up, though, I saw the parallels and differences between the two dead women I'd learned about today.

Marcos's reaction of violence stemmed from disrespect to his wife's memory and hurt toward his young children. His fury came from guilt and loss.

Ozias had lost his lover, and her murder incited him to lash out with vows of revenge. There was no guilt for not protecting her, but there was a need to blame and exact vengeance.

However, it revealed he cared for someone other than himself.

Which way would I react?

I shook my head and pushed open the door to my suite.

I had to marry Avra first, then answer the torrent of questions running through my mind.

Damn woman haunted me, and we'd barely spent any time together.

I needed to focus on why she wanted to marry me in the first place. No one offered themselves up on a platter to the son of their enemy without a reason.

If she believed I played by anyone else's rules instead of my own, she would be in for a rude awakening.

Six

vra

I fisted my hand as I stared at my reflection in the mirror. After a month of planning and preparation, according to Ozias's preferences, the day was here.

My wedding day.

This wasn't what I imagined as a little girl.

I miss you, Mama. I need your guidance, Papa.

I could only hope somewhere in heaven, Mama forgave me for marrying the son of her murderer. Papa, on the other hand, would understand this decision.

Out of all of us, I was most like him.

My parents ingrained family loyalty and honor into us, and there were no lengths we wouldn't go to seek justice.

However, at moments like this, regardless of who I married, I felt their absence as if the wounds that never truly healed were tearing open again. My dreams of Mama helping me dress with Laya and Cali talking nonstop would never happen. And no matter how much I wished it, Papa wasn't alive to walk me down the aisle.

I inhaled deeply, refusing to lose myself in the pain. I had worked so hard to control my emotions. As Vik always told me, I should use them to fuel my plans for the future.

Plus, my beautiful sisters, smarter than I ever could be, stood by me.

Through the walls of the ready room of the church, I heard the hum of noise, indicating the final preparations for the wedding.

The planner Ozias had hired was the only positive aspect of this situation. She attended to every detail and kept Ozias away from me. Her ability to maneuver people made me want to hire her for the Vitalis world.

I slid a hand down my body, admiring my dress. The planner had also introduced me to a local up-and-coming designer with exquisite taste. The gorgeous gown I'd chosen incorporated traditional Greek designs with high-fashion trends seen on the runway.

Of course, Ozias had interfered in the process, claiming the dress was too simple and cheap. He expected me to select something from the options *his* people chose, something too revealing.

The old man was out of his mind if he thought I would

let him sexualize me and make me nothing but a sexy trophy on his son's arm.

The gown I should have had on had disappeared in the aftermath of the coup. It had been passed down from generation to generation on my mother's side of the family to the firstborn daughter.

I would have altered it to fit me and fashioned it to something more to my taste, but the legacy the women of my family created would have continued.

Now, it was gone to who knew where, most likely burned or thrown out by the greedy bastard about to become my father-in-law.

"You're stunning," Cali said, jolting me away from the detour of anger where my thoughts were leading me.

She approached me from behind and smoothed a fold in my skirt.

I smiled and nodded. "This is definitely a showstopper. That idiot needs to learn that a lady can draw attention without displaying her goods."

The fabric hugged my every curve, and with the way the lace overlay avoided revealing too much skin, it gave the right amount of sexy.

"You look tall, elegant, and anything but Elias Xenos's inferior." The way Cali stated things brought a grin to my lips.

"I couldn't agree more. Elias is taller than me. There is no denying this fact. However, with these heels and my above-average height, I am at least near eye level with him." I took the lipstick Laya handed me to touch up my makeup and said, "I do love this dress."

"You look *amazing* in it," Laya agreed as she checked her hair in another mirror, glancing at me through the reflection. "How are you feeling about this? You can change your mind."

I lifted my shoulders, making sure the bodice of my dress could move with me.

"Can she?" Cali asked. "All of us are in too far to change the path. Just don't fall in love with him."

The youngest of the three of us was the most logical and felt the most. Cali would deny the latter until she was blue in the face, saying she knew how to control her emotions, but Laya and I knew her. She carried the empathy that had never bloomed in us.

"First, love is the last thing on my mind. This is a means to an end. Second, it doesn't matter how I feel." I nodded to my sisters. "We will avenge our family."

"I feel so bad, though." Cali stood, brushing down the creamy blue dress she'd chosen as my bridesmaid.

Oh, Cali, there she went, feeling too much.

"We agreed. We follow the plan."

Cali sighed. "I don't know if I'll ever stop feeling guilty about how you're...you're just sacrificing yourself like this."

Sacrificial lamb for the big, bad wolf. Elias's words returned to me, and I held back a scoff. "Don't worry, Cali. I'll be fine."

Why had my words sounded like a bad omen?

In the back of my mind, an uneasiness grew, not about the plan but that unsettling attraction to Elias.

I never responded to anyone the instant I met them, but it had happened with him.

Since that dinner with him and his father, I could not shake the memories of how he'd known just how to push me to lose my composure. His dominance seemed to incite a side of me to fight with him. When he'd warned me not to play with him, my immediate reaction was that he'd thrown down a challenge.

Then there was the fact that I kept thinking of his lips and wanting a taste of them.

How could such a brief interaction leave me in this confused state?

From the start, my sisters and I understood that the plan demanded we become wives in every sense of the word, including intimacy. We agreed to feign it, just as countless women had throughout the ages.

However, something deep in my gut told me nothing with Elias would go as planned.

"We'll all be fine," Laya said in a no-nonsense way. "Because we're back for what is ours, and no one will take it from us again."

"Soon," I told my sisters, "everyone will regret stealing from us."

The former Vitalis territories and land remained under our names despite other families taking over the area, completely unaware that Papa began dividing his assets long before anything happened to him. At each of our births,

Papa transferred ownership of parts of his estate into trusts for us. Most of what our enemies believed they'd taken as spoils of their plot against Juno Vitalis had legally never belonged to them. Even after marriage, what belonged to us remained ours. And if anything were to happen to one of us sisters, our trust would be divided between the remaining sisters or left to the next-in-line Vitalis to take over the family.

Papa had understood the ways of the world long before the deceit that resulted in his death.

It made no sense that no one in the last fifteen years had bothered to research the deeds and records for the land upon which they lay their heads. Or perhaps Ozias had, which was why he had so readily agreed to this marriage. Before he'd known I was alive, he knew the members of the Vitalis family in America were the only ones with the power to challenge him, and they were too busy expanding their reach locally to put effort into Europe.

As an extra precaution, before leaving Prague, my sisters and I had created wills stating upon our deaths, all of our assets would transfer to the Vitalis cousins in America.

Their support and loyalty to Papa meant more to me than they could know. I'd never forget their help with sorting through the lies of the past to unearth the facts about my parents' deaths.

Unfortunately, they couldn't attend the wedding due to issues in their territories. Having *some* family would have been a nice show of force, but it was what it was.

"You've got that right," Laya agreed with an unladylike grunt.

"I hate that we have to see those bastards today." Cali clenched her jaw.

Many of Ozias's co-conspirators planned to attend the wedding, especially the three who helped him mastermind everything. Inside the church would be a sea of enemies with a sprinkling of Vitalis soldiers as the few friendly faces.

"We have to hide our contempt," Laya advised as she came to my side, looking into the mirror before adding, "No matter how hard it may be."

"Yeah. Wear your cold, infallible mask," Cali added.

It was time to implement Vik's training and slide on the shield impenetrable to our enemies.

Except, they wouldn't get the unemotional part today. They would glimpse what simmered underneath.

I shook my head. "No. I want them to see the wrath in my eyes. It doesn't matter if they underestimate me or laugh at me. What they will know is that I am coming for them."

Laya's lips curved up on one side as she shook her head. "Then let's get this going."

Without any more delays or worries about how this would turn out, we filed out of the room and took our places in the procession.

I pushed back the thoughts of my parents and all the broken dreams and tucked my arm into Vik's.

The music commenced as I carefully walked down the aisle of the ancient church. The streamers, flowers, and vases of candles created a soft glow. The intricate details of the decor around me blurred my focus on the altar where the tall groom stood watching me.

A tingle shot down my spine, and goosebumps prickled my skin.

Elias's gaze locked on mine. He wore a well-cut and tailored tuxedo, accentuating his muscular body. His slicked-back salt-and-pepper hair accentuated his face's sharp, lean lines. He held himself like a mighty Greek god, a dominant, unapologetic killer.

Vik kissed my cheek once we reached the altar. There was a second of hesitation before he placed my hand over Elias's and stepped back.

A sweeping shift of emotions played through his eyes. Sadness. Pride. Love. Worry.

Vik gave me over to the enemy, but deep down, he believed in me.

He'd reminded me earlier in the morning to remember this was an act, only a sham, a necessary step in the plan.

No matter the game, Elias and I were entering a real marriage. He was the last lover I would ever take. I wasn't a cheater, and hell would freeze over before I looked the other way while anyone stepped out on me. Nothing outside of death ended this.

His dark-brown gaze narrowed as if he heard my thoughts. The power staring at me shouldn't appeal. He meant to taunt and intimidate. With others, it may work, but not with me.

I was a Vitalis.

I gave over my power to no one. Not to Elias and definitely not to his father.

The days of anyone lording over me were over. Cloe

learned this at the end of my pistol, and soon, I'd show this side to others.

The energy between Elias and me crackled, charging the air with challenge and anticipation. The aching desire that smoldered in the pit of my stomach from our initial meeting ignited into a low burning need.

Damn this attraction. I refused to succumb to the nuisance of a handsome face or intense dark eyes. However, the throbbing between my legs and the flood of arousal coursing through me said otherwise.

I barely knew this man, and I definitely couldn't trust him. But sure as fuck, my body responded to him and wanted him in the worst possible way.

"Are you ready to become the wolf's dinner, Avra?" he asked in a deep, intoxicating tone.

The heat of his large hand seeped into mine as he guided me toward the priest.

As we knelt, I whispered, "Perhaps I'm the wolf, and you're my dinner."

"I'm counting on it." He lifted my knuckles to his lips and brushed a kiss against them.

By all the saints, this man was potent. What had I gotten myself into?

The wedding commenced as if in a blur. The vows went in one ear and out the other. I simply followed along with the cues, making sure to play my role of the seemingly demure and patient bride.

My family knew it was an act, and Elias had apparently seen through the guise. However, the rest of the attendants accepted the ruse as I performed the steps of the old traditions until I left the one-hundred-year-old building as a married woman.

My composure nearly slipped during the ring exchange. I had told Vik to handle the details of selecting the band for Elias, thinking he wouldn't care as long as it wasn't gaudy.

Except when Elias slowly and delicately slipped my ring onto my finger, I could only stare at it in awe.

It was breathtaking and something I'd have chosen for myself under different circumstances. The artistry of the design made it unique, and the stones weren't so big that it made me look as if he owned me, but large and prominent enough to state my unavailable status. I never expected a Xenos to pick a ring like this.

Again, he'd read my thoughts and responded, "We share blood but aren't the same, little wolf."

Before I realized it, the ceremony ended. "You may now kiss your bride."

The traditional wording. Their possessiveness implied I would be Elias's, not that he'd be mine or that we'd be each other's.

I shook the thought away and waited to see if Elias actually planned to kiss me. Nothing with him had gone as expected. Why would this?

His focus landed on my lips, almost like a physical caress, and they tingled in response. I took in an unsteady breath, and immediately, his expression darkened.

As if in slow motion, he cupped my face. The branding

of his hold and the heat of his touch shot through me, and without thought, I leaned toward him.

I kept my eyes on him as he dropped his mouth to mine. Desire spiked through me, a tingling from head to toe. It was the barest, briefest brush of his mouth against mine, too short and too tender, but a knowing settled over me.

The kiss sealed my fate to his in more ways than marriage. One of us would fall, one would break, and one would hurt the other.

I went still, unable to let him see how much the realization had the back of my throat burning.

As he stepped back, still holding my hand with the ring he'd given me, his expression revealed he was as unsettled as I was.

SEVEN

vra

I found myself at the periphery of a crowd gathered in what used to be a lovely enclosed garden veranda belonging to my family. Now, it showcased only the ostentatious displays of an insecure man longing for validation and eager to assert his dominance in the hierarchy of influence and wealth.

Even after fifteen years, Ozias Xenos refused to accept that one could show power without shoving it in the faces of others. You embodied it, lived it, and carried it.

My gaze settled on Elias, who stood in the center of a group of European and American syndicate heads invited for the occasion. They were in the middle of an animated discussion.

The business and politics of our world never ceased, even during a wedding. Elias seemed fully engaged in the conversation in front of him. Yet, something about his posture indicated that he was aware of everyone around him.

Especially me.

From the moment we left the church, we barely exchanged more than a dozen words with each other, even during the couple's dance. Yet, in that moment, staying silent was for the best. The unspoken attraction between us pulsed as if it were a living thing, making it clear that the sex to come would be far from gentle.

Shit, this wasn't the time for that train of thought.

In the next instant, my gaze locked with Elias's. It was disconcerting how we seemed to sense each other, whether across the large room or within reach.

Perhaps it was a blessing that the activities of the wedding reception kept us busy, playing Ozias's puppets as he showboated as the actual guest of honor.

The proud papa who bagged a Vitalis for his son.

He wanted this moment, so be it.

And from the way Elias shook his head every time he noticed his father's antics, he made clear he believed Ozias the fool for the behavior he displayed.

Ozias's roar of laughter boomed out throughout the room, and I muttered, "Idiot."

"Naughty, naughty," Laya said with a smirk as she approached. "Don't let anyone else catch you displaying disgust at your father-in-law's need for attention."

"This isn't my wedding. It's his."

Laya shrugged. "You were aware of this going in."

"Seeing it on display is different. The man is an older version of the 'pick me' boy."

"I can't believe you said that." Laya laughed. "I'm happy Cali didn't hear it, or she would only add fuel to that fire."

I spotted her across the room with Vik, who looked as if he were giving Cali a lecture of some type. "I can only assume she is sharing her views with Vik at the moment."

"At least she only gives her opinions to us. I was proud of everyone for keeping calm during the photography session and throughout dinner."

"The spectacle of it all is nauseating. I keep reminding myself all of this is for a purpose."

"Yes, to avenge our family and take back what belongs to us."

"The home we knew no longer exists, Laya. Look around you. He destroyed the simple beauty of it. Elias said we won't have to spend a night under the same roof as that bastard."

"At least you have that."

"I'm not sure I'd want to stay here even if he lived somewhere else."

Laya's lips tightened as rage washed over her features, then just as fast calmed before she set a hand on my arm. "Our memories will always belong to us. A home is what we make. Once we achieve our goal, we will rebuild and preserve what is left."

"That is something we can look forward to in our future. One of the many prizes at the end of our mission."

Laya scanned the room. "Eventually, the masses will tire and make their departures."

I smirked this time. "I wouldn't count on it. They are all gawking at us. I can guarantee they still haven't recovered from the shock of our survival or the fact we have returned fifteen years later. They expect something volatile to happen."

The room buzzed with conversation, and many of the people gathered were familiar to us. We knew of them or had interacted with them. Some had even been kind to us as children. Then, there were women similar in age to me and my sisters, whom we once considered friends. They were nothing but strangers now.

Many shot us glances and only a few approached us to speak and rekindle acquaintances.

"If I were in their place, my anticipation level would sit at a thousand." Laya pressed her hand to her chest in mock expectation. "Think about it. While we hid, our enemies grew richer off our territories. Now, you marry the son of the man who orchestrated the demise of our family. This is entertainment at its finest."

"Want to help me give them a show?" I lasered onto three individuals who deserved as painful deaths as Ozias.

They had pretended to be Papa's allies, took the wealth he brought to them, and then betrayed him. With my new father-in-law, they'd stolen and carved up what was rightfully Vitalis territory. What was my sisters' territory. *My* territory.

Cristo Caras. Morisi Bella. Pello Korba.

For years, I'd repeated their names like a mantra.

And here they were right before me, the marked men.

Laya turned, shifting her attention behind her. "I wouldn't dream of denying you the pleasure of poking at them. You are the Vitalis, after all."

Laya's words settled over me.

I was the Vitalis, the eldest in the family, the one to bear the title.

I headed the family and represented it.

"You are correct. I'll go say hello."

"And I will warn Vik. Good thing he packed the place with Vitalis soldiers so no one gets any ideas."

I worked my way through the crowd, my focus on the men laughing and talking without a care in the world, enjoying the fruits of what was created by Vitalis hands.

It sickened me how they enjoyed the wedding of the woman whose family they helped tear apart.

My rage ripped through me, ready to unleash. The desire to shoot them right here, in front of everyone, clawed at my nerves and incited every one of my dark desires.

As I moved in closer, I pulled every ounce of hatred back, reminding the anger fighting inside me of the goal.

I wouldn't lose control and give the bastards anything over me.

Fuck every last one of them.

As I neared, Pello Korba lifted his hand, inviting Elias to join the men. Seeing him drawn into the circle with my enemies fueled my agitation.

He knew my history with those three. But then again, his father led their group.

Why had he agreed to marry me when he questioned my motives from the very beginning?

What was in it for him? Perhaps he simply enjoyed a life full of trouble. Or he was one of those sick fucks who like pain and misery and hardship.

Even if Ozias had demanded his son to marry, no one could force a man like Elias to do anything. I'd met enough hard men to recognize he was one. A ruthless, impatient man who bent for no one.

Elias had his reasons to marry me.

And I planned to learn what they were.

Lingering in the background, I plucked a drink from a server and sipped, biding my time until Elias left.

After a few minutes, he stepped away to speak with one of his men, and I moved in with precise deliberation.

These men couldn't intimidate me. They'd aged well. For men only in their late fifties or sixties, they look far younger. Then again, with their wealth and resources, they possessed the means to stay healthy and fit.

Cristo Caras noticed my approach first and raised his nearly empty glass to me. "Ah, here comes the bride."

"Congratulations," Pello cheered, slurring his speech.

I stepped right up to them, calm and relaxed, without revealing the actual depth of my loathing for them.

Keeping my champagne flute pinched loosely between my fingers, I held my head high and gave them no response to their praise for the wedding.

"I'm so proud of you," Morisi Bella said, grinning widely.

"If your father were here to see the gorgeous little woman you are..."

Pello laughed, shaking his head at his friend's ill choice of words.

"It's a perfect match," Cristo boomed over Morisi's not-so-secret dig. "You will bear Elias fine children."

Assholes. All of them.

I wouldn't rush this. I had to wait, listen, endure the idiots' stupid fawning.

None of them wanted the best for me and Elias, or Ozias. They sought to protect themselves and played the game.

Silent and patient, I stood there. They weren't even aware of the lack of conversation on my part.

Finally, when I had had enough of their self-flattery and nostalgic conversation, I broke the festive mood. "Cut the bullshit."

They fell silent, giving me astonished, stern glares.

Was their surprise because of my directness or the fact a female dared to speak to them in such a manner?

"None of you wants me or my sisters around."

Cristo furrowed his brow while the other two clenched their jaws. Not one of them dared to deny it.

At least they were honest enough to keep from lying about that.

"Were you surprised we survived?" I stepped one foot closer, pushing my shoulders back and standing as tall and proud as possible. "I know you hate it. We are the reminder of your past. You know, the one you do everything to wash away and pretend never happened."

Pello opened his mouth, but I wasn't in the mood to hear him and cut him off. "I have no time for lectures. "I'm here to tell you to expect notices. The landlord disapproves of squatters."

"How dare you threaten us," Morisi said, snapping out of his stunned silence, outrage on his face as he crowded me.

His height couldn't intimidate me. I wasn't the little girl of fifteen years ago.

I was the Vitalis.

Fuck him to think to use his size to frighten me.

I lifted my chin to him. "I never threatened you once. I never raised my voice and only relayed a message. You are the one taking a threatening stance as weak men do against women they can't control."

He stepped back as he realized his behavior had garnered attention from those around us.

Cursing under his breath, he shook his head and turned to Pello. "This brat comes back only to start trouble."

"You created the trouble when you betrayed my parents." I paused to look each of them in the eyes. "And it is something that I will never let you forget."

"You better watch what—"

I lifted my hand in Pello's face, cutting off his retort. "For over one hundred and fifty years, the Vitalis has been in power. And that won't change anytime soon."

Cristo scoffed, smirking. "Your family isn't in power anymore. They haven't been for years."

"What you've done is nothing more than a minor hiccup in our history. Being in charge is relative."

"Relative?" Pello snarled, chuckling with malice. "Being in charge is something you'll never know about, girl."

Oh, he wanted to force a reaction from me. "Keep believing whatever you want. Just know this little girl has no fear of you. I see you. I see all of you. Remember, your landlord is coming."

"Being Ozias's daughter-in-law gives you no power. Don't think otherwise," Morisi stated and then laughed. "He's the one you should warn. You are no match for us."

One by one, they gave in to laughter, mocking me with their chuckles and sneers.

"Go ahead and underestimate me, gentlemen." I gave them a smile meant to taunt. "Just know, in the end, only one of us will remain, and it's the one with ovaries."

EIGHT

E^{lias}

I drank down a hefty swallow of whiskey after finishing another conversation with a well-wisher at the reception and moved to the periphery of the room. This entire day was nothing but an excuse for Ozias to flaunt his wealth, our rivals and friends to mingle and keep track of each other, and the elite of society to find new gossip.

It was a production, a finely tuned machine made of many cogs and wheels working together to give the impression that Avra and I were the quintessential couple heading into a life of matrimony with all the well-wishes and congratulations we could ever want.

It couldn't end fast enough so Avra and I could escape.

Barely a second after I'd kissed Avra on the altar, I'd fought the urge to lay my mouth on her plump lips again and devour her. That brief taste had set to life a craving I needed to satisfy.

And for me to accomplish any of my carnal goals, it required privacy, something unavailable to me until this whole charade ended.

I planned to take my time with Avra, on her mouth with her sharp, clever tongue. I had a fascinating need to explore and taste every part of her. Sex with one woman for the rest of my life never appealed before, but I had a feeling it might with Avra.

There was no chance of doing anything with this joke of a reception, where I stood around receiving nonstop praise and congratulations.

The dinner and the couple's dance exacerbated my annoyance at this display of excess. Having her in my arms and watching the flush creep up her skin sparked a caveman desire to throw her over my shoulder, take her to my suite of rooms, and consummate this marriage.

Instead, we avoided any conversation and made as much eye contact as possible.

Now, here I lingered, ready for another tumbler of whiskey to maintain the pretense the Xenos family ruled this section of Greece.

But I knew better, as did everyone else.

With Avra's return, with her sisters here in the room, the tide prepared to change.

The shock of seeing them healthy, strong, and very much

alive rippled throughout not only the attendees of the wedding but also the entire territory, if not Greece.

The Vitalises were royalty with ties to the old ways of our world.

Anyone who studied the sisters would see the unmasked intelligence in their eyes. They were every inch Juno Vitalis's daughters, cunning and dangerous.

Especially the one that was mine.

Mine.

I couldn't help but smile. I had married a beautiful predator, a perfect match for someone like me. I couldn't wait until she learned I could hold my own with her.

Setting my empty glass on a counter, I searched for Avra.

Instead of her, I saw another woman who shouldn't be here.

Francesca.

The blond glided through the guests, mingling near the ice fountain. The fact she hadn't been invited and seeing her here incited suspicion about her motives.

Her focus landed on me, and I braced for some type of altercation. It looked as if she still refused to accept our association was over.

Immediately after the engagement became official, I broke things off with Francesca. She hadn't taken the news well, begging me to reconsider and stooping so low as to offer to keep things as they were. She proposed to continue an affair after I married Avra.

There wasn't any pondering my response, so I declined. Unlike my father, I wasn't a cheater.

This only caused her to sob, wail, beg, and pray.

She changed her tactics when she realized I wouldn't bend, accusing me of using her. I'd used her body just as she had mine. She knew marriage wasn't part of our arrangement from the beginning. If she thought otherwise, then that was on her.

Her eyes brightened as she drew near, but I passed her, taking a different route and giving her a wide berth.

That was when I spotted Avra speaking with Cristo Caras, Morisi Bella, and Pello Korba. They were Ozias's closest allies and the co-conspirators who'd helped him create the situation for Juno Vitalis's murder in the middle of the city.

Those were the last men I expected her to be with. The cold anger blazing in her eyes as she spoke told me she'd rather set them on fire than look at them.

And from the angry scowls on the men's faces, they were no fans of hers.

"What the fuck," I growled.

It wasn't as if I was unaware of her ulterior motives for our marriage. At least she could have waited until after the reception to start poking her enemies.

These men weren't known for logic or reasoning. They acted before thinking and then regretted their actions.

I rushed over, curious and impatient to see what was happening and drawing nearer in time to catch bits of their discussion.

"Being in charge is something you'll never know about, girl."

"Keep believing whatever you want. Just know, this little girl has no fear of you." Avra pointed from her eyes to theirs and then said in a calm, almost melodic voice, "I see you. I see all of you. Remember, your landlord is coming."

"Being Ozias's daughter-in-law gives you no power. Don't think otherwise," Morisi stated. "He's the one you should warn. You are no match for us."

The men laughed, mocking Avra. Her expression remained serene.

"Go ahead and underestimate me, gentlemen." She gave an exaggerated sigh and then shrugged. "Just know, in the end, only one of us will remain, and it's the one with ovaries."

For fuck's sake.

Each of the men lost their smiles and laughter.

Their expressions fell, crumbling as they stared at her heated vow. I had to defuse the situation—*now*. This wasn't the time or place for this kind of complicated confrontation. And it looked like my new wife couldn't have cared less about when or where she made her thoughts known to them.

I quickened my steps, coming up behind her. Even if she registered my presence behind her, she gave no outward acknowledgment, only holding the angry death glares of the men with her cool, unaffected one.

She showed no apparent reaction as I wrapped my arm around her waist, sliding it along her back and side. I drew her back, and a jolt of awareness struck me, but I fought to ignore how right she felt against me.

With me.

Once we were alone, I anticipated a scolding for interrupting her. Still, she had no idea the danger she was treading in.

Cristo barely glanced at me, keeping his sneer firmly in place as Avra settled her palm over my hand. "You think you're so smart."

"There is no think in that equation. It is a fact."

My hold on her tightened. Why couldn't she keep quiet?

"Here is some truth," Morisi added. "The wisdom of leaving the past in the past is best for your health and your sisters'."

The muscles in Avra's back tensed, and the anger in her radiated out. She turned toward me and lifted her hand, placing it on my chest. Fire burned in her eyes as she stared up at me.

It was my turn to step in.

So that was her game.

This was all about putting on a show and letting everyone see how seamlessly we fit together as a couple, fake smiles and forced touches and all.

I knew if I remained quiet longer than necessary, nothing would stop Avra from rendering another stinging retort.

I shifted, aligning my position with Avra's. "Then can I assume the three of you learned from the past and plan to leave it there?"

I held each man's gaze as I spoke the last few words. "There were many mistakes. Ones that no one plans to repeat."

I tugged Avra closer to me, almost hugging her with the

urgency I felt about pulling her out of this situation. There was no de-escalating the tension she'd built against them.

I had to get her the hell out of here. But first, I needed to ensure Ozias's cronies understood my statement.

"Isn't that right, gentlemen?" I asked them, daring them to argue with my advice.

Cristo grunted, lifting his glass to his lips before realizing it was empty.

"Sure," Morisi agreed. "Sure, sure. The past stays in the past."

That wasn't what I fucking said.

"Congrats," Pello replied, avoiding any acknowledgment of my words regarding old mistakes.

All three gave the impression of agreement while meaning none of it. They regretted nothing. To them, Juno Vitalis had made all the mistakes by trusting them. They were just like Ozias, possessing not a single ounce of remorse for their actions.

Greedy bastards, all of them, drunk on power and full of egos. I couldn't wait to unseat them. Slitting their throats one by one would be a bonus.

Avra stiffened in my arms as the men turned away. Her rigid posture warned me that her temper had yet to cool.

I doubted she'd appreciate how I'd come in and taken over her conversation. I had known she disliked anyone talking over her from our first dinner, but there had been no other option here. The fact she knew when to give over to me said she understood the politics of this, even if she hated every moment of it.

As she turned to me slightly, fisting her fingers on my shirt, I wondered what would happen if she ever released the torrent of anger she locked away inside.

She bunched the fabric with a trembling rage, even though the relaxed expression on her flawless face gave the impression of peace and serenity.

"There will always be consequences for one's actions," she uttered darkly.

I knew she was talking about my statement to the men. If she wasn't happy with my handling of the situation, I couldn't give a rat's ass.

It was time for her to deal with me.

"Very true." I hugged her closer. "Your actions have them as well."

Before she could say anything, I rushed her out of the large room.

"Are you out of your mind?"

Ignoring her protests, I guided her through the crowd and to the back of the house into one of the receiving rooms, far enough away from the guests to avoid an audience.

She wrenched herself free from my grip, breathless and radiating fury. "You asshole. What is your problem?"

She wasn't the only one pissed off.

"What the fuck were you thinking?" I resisted the urge to yell. "You're the one out of your mind. How could you confront people like them at our wedding?"

I locked the door, not wanting to chance anyone walking in.

"Oh." She crossed her arms and jutted one hip out. "I'm

supposed to be the meek, silent wife? The fool who smiles at them and lets them—"

"Yes," I growled, keeping my voice down. "Those three don't think before they act. They will put a hit on you for something as minor as insulting their ego, not caring you're my wife."

I stalked toward her. Instead of retreating, she stood her ground as if daring me.

The damn woman was infuriating.

"I will not apologize."

"I'm not stupid. I wasn't asking you to."

"Then don't expect me just to roll over and be happy that the very people who killed my father showed up to my wedding."

"Like you give a fuck about the wedding. About marrying me. It's just a play. Just an act, and don't try to tell me otherwise."

She slammed her lips together even tighter, and the sight of her so mad, so riled up, so *alive*, tempted me to take out my outrage on her the way I'd wanted earlier.

Fucking her into submission might be easier than getting her to listen to logic.

"It doesn't matter. They had no right to come here today, representing the families who ruined mine."

I gritted my teeth, reaching out for her but knowing that'd be my first mistake. With how furious I was and how deeply she taunted me.

I knew that the second I touched her I wouldn't want to

stop. "You married into one of those families. They are my father's allies. So you need to get used to it."

She lifted her hands, shoving at me and growing angrier when I wouldn't budge. I gripped her hands and brought her nose to nose with me.

We stared each other down, our breaths unsteady.

"It doesn't mean I have to like it."

I squeezed her wrists, wishing I could shake some sense into her. Or some answers out of her.

"Why did you want to marry me, Avra?"

She tipped her chin up, stubbornly silent.

"Why?" I demanded again. "What is it you gain by marrying me?"

Her laughter bubbled up, low and dark, as she smirked at me. "Isn't it obvious after that scene?"

I moved closer, refusing to heed this raging desire that Avra's rebelliousness, her defiance, spawned in me.

I stepped forward, setting one foot between her braced ones, our bodies close enough to brush. I resisted this electric tension that consumed me every second she pushed back.

"Spell it out for me," I ordered.

She leaned up, bringing her lips to my ear.

"Revenge," she replied.

I reared back, shaking my head. Still holding her wrists, I kept her close as I looked her in the eye. "That was a grave error on your part. I'm not the type of man to be led around by my dick. If that's what you planned, it won't happen."

She yanked her hands free and slapped me. As the sting

spread over my skin, I stared down at her, the outrage etched over her features.

"I'm not some whore," she shot back.

"You're wrong." I lurched forward, grabbing her and pinning her to the wall behind her back.

She panted, sheer violence radiating out from her. She lifted her hand, clenching it as if to punch me, but I grabbed it and her other one, trapping them above her head.

"Let me go, you asshole."

"I'm not an asshole. I'm your husband."

"Same thing," she seethed.

"I brought you in here to have the actions and consequences discussion. However, you need a demonstration."

"Don't you dare." Her chest heaved with hard breaths, pushing her breasts against me.

"Dare what? Fuck you? Make you my whore?"

"I said I wasn't a whore."

"But you are. You are my whore. My wife. Mine to do with as I please."

A flush crept up her cheeks, and lust glittered in her eyes, replacing the volcanic rage.

Through clenched teeth, she said, "Keep dreaming, Eli."

I grinned, liking how she'd shortened my name, something only the few closest to me ever used.

"No dreams needed. It's reality." I brought my face a hairsbreadth from hers. "You will submit."

"No." She held my gaze, pupils dilating and challenge in her eyes. "Never to a Xenos."

This back-and-forth sparring aroused her as much as it

infuriated her. Avra wasn't a woman to allow anyone to dominate her, and now here she was, pinned against a wall with me looming over her.

I lowered one hand, gliding it down the column of her neck, and gripped her throat. "You married a Xenos. That makes you one. It labels you as mine."

"Never," she growled, jerking against my hold even though she knew struggling was useless.

I wouldn't let her go.

"Mine," I repeated in a dark growl.

She continued to thrash until she accepted there was no freedom for her.

Breathing heavily, she remained quiet, only glaring at me with loathing and volatile hunger.

The blood in my veins heated, pushing at the rabid animal inside to take this woman and make her mine.

Her focus shifted to my mouth before she closed her eyes and muttered, "Fuck, I so hate you."

"The feeling is mutual," I groaned right as I slammed my mouth to hers.

Nine

E lias

She moaned, not protest or resistance, but pure need and desire. This woman wouldn't shy away from demanding what she wanted.

It incited a craving in me to make her beg, scream, admit she was mine.

I grazed my teeth over her lower lip, just hard enough to sting and eliciting a filthy, wanton gasp as she arched against me.

"You are *my* whore now," I whispered with a guttural rawness I couldn't hide. "Do you hear me?"

She swallowed without losing that scowl. Her face said

she hated me, despised me, but the gritty lust in her seductive green eyes told me otherwise. I felt her throat strain with the motion of her muscles there.

Physically, my strength outmatched hers tenfold, something that would never change.

And then there were the rules of our world. The men ran things, and adjusting that mindset would take decades, if not more, no matter how defiant and opinionated she was.

"You have such soft, unmarred, flawless skin." My scarred, tatted, calloused hand flexed on her delicate neck painted a heady contrast to the flesh under my fingers.

"Do you plan to mark it? Brand me as yours?" She arched her throat.

The desire to harm her wouldn't ever enter my mind.

She was mine. To protect. To fuck. To literally do with as I pleased, but hurting her wasn't something to ever consider.

Why she challenged me, knowing I'd killed so many, beaten and tortured many more, was an enigma to explore.

My capacity for violence and malice scared so many. Yet, Avra's green eyes blazed with lust, defiance, and not a single drop of fear.

Fucking woman captivated me. She trusted me, knowing my father had killed her mother.

Well, at least with her body, she did.

I squeezed tighter as I smashed my mouth to hers. Avra's hot, wet lips parted, welcoming my brutal, commanding kiss. The second I speared my tongue into her mouth, she met me with her own demands.

The taste of her intoxicated me as if she were a witch. She

growled and turned slightly, ending the kiss with a nip on the lip harder than necessary and meant to cause pain.

I hissed, tightening my fingers.

Her lips curved, and her pupils dilated, watching me lick the blood from my lips.

"I'm not your *whore*," she stated. "I'm no one's whore."

"What are you?" I asked with a gravelly laugh as I rubbed my bleeding mouth to hers.

She'd drawn it, she'd taste it.

She sucked my lip into her mouth, surprising me by licking over the cut, and then said, "I'm your *wife*."

Fuck, I liked the sound of that.

My wife.

This fiery woman belonged to me and no one else.

I had no doubt this moment set a precedent for our future, one filled with fights full of passion and taunts, never simple or tame.

A man like me needed someone who wouldn't crumble when I pushed back.

"It's the same fucking thing from where I stand." I brushed my lips over hers in slow passes, tasting them and teasing them just enough to elicit a response before pulling away.

She couldn't reach up toward me, not with my hand on her throat and the other pinning her wrist over her head. I had her right where I wanted her, vulnerable and ripe for the taking.

"You won't win this," I taunted, bringing my mouth a fraction from hers. "Your body's reactions tell me you want to fuck. You don't want something sweet and gentle. No, that won't do for you."

"Stop talking and kiss me."

I smirked right before taking her lips and devouring her mouth. Her body arched as if trying to get closer, and her tongue dueled with mine, meeting my demands with hers.

Those moans. Desperate, needy growls and mewls, wordless pleas and whimpers for more. It was music to my ears.

"You're my fucking whore, Avra," I repeated.

Still, she shook her head, refusing to agree. She wouldn't meet my gaze until I tipped her chin up higher and forced her to face me.

"You're mine to hold. To keep." I flexed my fingers around her throat and pushed my hips against her, grinding her against the wall. Her breath hitched at the friction of my cock, rubbing right where she needed it the most.

"To kiss." I did, biting her chin this time.

"To fuck." Releasing her neck, I grabbed a handful of her dress and yanked it up.

The desire to tear the fucking thing off her rode me, but I couldn't ruin the garment. Damn social responsibility and returning to our guests.

However, underwear wasn't a requirement.

"You're my whore now," I growled against the warm skin of her neck right before kissing and sucking it.

"Never."

I couldn't get enough of her taste, her smooth sweetness.

In reality, she wasn't sweet. Instead, fire burned in her

blood. Even so, something about her made it so I couldn't get enough of her.

These were too many fucking clothes.

I wanted her bare, to explore every tight inch of her body.

Later, I planned to touch until I filled this need. This insatiable want made no sense. The insanity, the feral necessity to mark Avra, take her.

I freed her hands and tugged down the neckline of her gown, loving the way her breasts spilled out, swaying as I ground my dick against her through the layers separating us.

Her clean, white dress scrunched up between us. She grappled for my tie, loosening it, and then fumbled with my shirt. Her breaths came in short pants, and her face flushed.

I held her in place against the wall.

"You'll take whatever I give you," I swore before I reached lower to grab the back of her thigh.

Her flesh was warm and smooth, so soft and firm with muscles. I pushed her thigh up and over, making room for myself. I fought the vision of her wrapping those legs around me as I pounded into her.

"You're going to take everything I give you," I ordered as I ran my hand farther up her leg. Beneath the layers of her dress, it was a blind exploration to reach her pussy. Still, the second I swiped my fingers through her dripping arousal, I growled and kissed her with a punishing bite once more. I snapped the thin band of her thong and slid my fingers deep inside her.

"Oh, God." She arched. "Just like that."

"You want more, don't you, my little whore?" Not

waiting for her to answer, I pushed in another digit and pressed my thumb against her clit.

The way her cunt dripped, there was no denying she preferred rough over gentle.

"You hear me?" I worked her, bringing her higher, and right before she reached her peak, I pulled out.

"Are you out of your mind? Don't stop."

This demonstration wasn't about pleasing her, about her comfort. This was about—

"What'd you say out there? Everyone's actions should have consequences?"

She hissed through clenched teeth, scowling at me as I kept my fingers from that tight hole I rimmed but wouldn't reenter.

She adjusted her hips, trying to dip lower and seek out my fingers, but she wasn't getting anything easy tonight.

This experience was a raw, dirty fucking, representative of my vicious need to claim her and teach her.

"Isn't that what you said?" I rasped as I shifted my pants to let my dick spring out.

"I said..." she uttered, panting so quickly and breathing heavily.

"Actions have consequences," I finished for her as I jerked her dress up some more. I notched the tip of my cock at her pussy. Rubbing into her juices, I grabbed her thigh and held it up to the wall.

"Actions. Like marrying me."

She nodded, subtly rocking her hips to mine. I wasn't blind to her desperate fidgeting. I was right there, ready to breach her tight heat. Already, the broad head of my dick stretched her slippery cunt.

"Marrying me has consequences," I said.

"Like taking your cock," she retorted, trying again to push against me and get me inside. "All talk and no—"

I slammed into her. With one brutal hard drive, I thrust into her slick pussy until I was in to the hilt. She sucked me in like a perfectly fitting glove. So fucking good. So tight. So hot. I strained to breathe through the need to pull out and pound back in.

She whimpered as she adjusted to my brutal drive into her. After all that push and pull. All that fighting and give or take. This was my reward. She'd wanted it, taunting me like that. Her thighs were slick with cream. She was wet, just as turned on as I was, but still, she froze in utter disbelief as I filled her so deep.

"Hold on." She gasped, dropping her head back against the wall. "I haven't done this in a while."

Annoyance crept up the back of my neck out of nowhere. Until now, until Avra, I never gave a shit about my lovers' pasts, but with Avra, I wanted to rip whoever she fucked before me to shreds.

Right now wasn't the time to focus on that. There were other things on the agenda.

"Marrying me has consequences like you being my whore." I slowly pulled back, loving the hot slide of her pussy wrapped around me.

Keeping only the tip of my dick inside, I tortured her, holding myself still, waiting until she squirmed for me to thrust back in. I repeated the moves until little mewled whimpers escaped her lips.

"You take my cock, like such a good little wife. Like such a good little whore." I slammed in harder, shoving her against the wall.

She gurgled, gasping in shock again. She held onto me tight, unable to do anything else. Her lids lowered, hooding those sparkling green orbs of pure need.

Again, I pulled out slowly, tormenting both of us.

"Like shutting up and letting me give you the fucking you've been begging for."

I gritted my teeth, thrusting into her harder and harder.

Her eyes closed shut as she moaned, and her pussy contracted and flexed, making my cock grow harder.

"Eli, I need."

"What is it you need?" I asked through clenched teeth.

Over and over, I pounded into her with a relentless force. I whipped my hips, pummeling her tight pussy.

"Right there. Oh. Right there." She dropped her forehead to mine.

I barely brushed my thumb across her clit, and she detonated, her back bowing and her nails digging into the skin of my nape.

"Eli," she cried out as her pussy clamped down as if it were a vise grip on my throbbing cock.

My control snapped, and without giving a damn about anyone hearing, I pushed her into the wall so hard that her back thudded. Each deep sink of my cock into her soaked cunt had her moaning louder. Every time I ground against her, rocking upward to get her to take all of my dick, she clenched me tighter. I wanted that orgasm to keep going.

It was perfect. It was filthy. It was a brutal taking.

Her release had barely faded when she slapped her hands to the wall, trying to push up and find purchase as I drove into her with a furious need to fill her with my cum.

I grabbed both of her hands and held them in place. She was almost spread-eagle against the surface of the wall as I fucked into her with all the pent-up anger and frustration I'd held in. She cried out.

Faster. Harder. Deeper. I lost myself in the need to come, to bruise Avra's pussy with the brutal hits of my body against hers. Pinned to the wall, rocking from my thrusts, she took it.

Like a good whore.

My whore.

"My wife," I uttered, almost in disbelief still that I had one.

In all her defiant, bold attitude, Avra was the woman who'd belong to me for the rest of our lives.

She sucked in a quick breath, clamping her tight pussy around me. She trembled and quivered, shaking as she came again.

I smashed my mouth to hers, muffling her unrestrained cries. Her orgasm was too much to resist. I was too close. I was right there. She was too tight and slick, wrapped around me and milking me so good.

Angling my face to lock us together, I drove into her without a break until I came. My balls had been so tight, high, and ready for me to come, and with a tingling streak of pleasure along my spine, I gave in and filled her womb with jet after jet of my cum.

Goosebumps covered my skin, and I resisted the chill of a shiver at how fucking good she was. At how damned heady a fuck against the wall could be with her. Pleasure coursed through me as I remained lodged deep inside her.

"I'm only your whore when we fuck, Eli," Avra said as she continued to catch her breath.

I lifted my head from her neck and looked at her. "Where else would you be my whore?"

"I want to make sure you understand I'm only this way in private. I submit to no one in public."

My cock twitched at the challenge in her green eyes. The need to fuck her again, to make her do as she'd said—submit—pulsed in my blood.

Except murmurs of voices, nearing, reached my ears, telling me someone was looking for us.

I pulled out of her.

"Our time alone is over." I stepped back and looked at her gown, almost cringing at its state.

Well, there was that saying about hell and good intentions for a reason.

Avra looked down at herself and sighed. "Well, it looks as if I will need an outfit change."

"Don't tell me you have an extra wedding dress lying around here."

"No. Laya expected me to tire of the layers of heavy material and packed an elegant alternative just in case."

I stared at her. "Something tells me your sisters and you make plans for your plans."

Her unguarded smile hit me in a way I wasn't sure I liked. But how it lit up her face and accentuated her beauty was worth it.

"Let's say the Vitalis women watch out for each other. Maybe one day you will garner an invitation into our circle."

TEN

I released a deep breath, unsure how to describe my first few weeks as a married woman. I rolled to my side on the bed and gazed out the window of Eli's estate home in the countryside. The warm weather and the blue sky gave the room a whimsical atmosphere, but life wasn't exactly that.

Most newlyweds would spend their days on an official honeymoon, except Eli and I weren't like other couples. This union was a business arrangement, not a marriage in the traditional sense. Honeymoons and time off with one's significant other weren't part of the equation.

Thankfully, Eli kept his promise and never forced me to stay a single night under the same roof as Ozias. When the wedding festivities ended, Eli swept me out of the city and took me to one of his other properties.

I watched the birds fly over the water and pulled the sheet tighter to my chest as a breeze filtered through the sheer curtains.

I planned to enjoy these few moments with myself before Eli charged out of the bathroom, expecting me to jump at his order to prepare for our return to Patras.

The man loved to boss me around, and of course, that meant I challenged him. Why I enjoyed doing or saying the opposite of everything he said or wanted made no damn sense. Maybe some twisted, sadistic part of me had decided to emerge and make its presence known.

Whatever it was, I couldn't get enough of his hands on me, and poking at him in some way or another got me fucked.

This couldn't be normal.

I winced and rolled to a sitting position before reaching for a glass of water on the side table and drinking the contents.

I studied Eli's packed suitcases and my open ones and shook my head. We'd barely spent more than a few nights in one place for nearly a month.

Work, work, work. It was all Eli did.

Then again, the family would run itself into the ground if Eli wasn't in charge. Ozias liked to play leader, but everyone at every estate knew Eli ran the Xenos family, from the controlling lieutenants to the vineyard workers.

The biggest surprise over this past month, outside of his

insistence we were never to sleep apart unless absolutely necessary, was that he wasn't bothered by my presence while he conducted business with his lieutenants.

I kept telling myself it was a mind game to trick me into dropping my guard and trusting him.

Eli ran things in a fashion that reminded me so much of Papa. His methods of managing the Xenos and Vitalis territories garnered respect and a bit of fear. There was no favoritism in his management. He expected results and wanted all under his watch to be thriving.

However, when it came to the private side of things, our relationship made no damn sense. We lived a pattern of arguing and fucking, with a little bit of getting to know each other thrown in on occasion.

Eli still wasn't over the whole thing about my confronting Cristo, Morisi, and Pello. Every chance possible, he voiced his frustration and irritation about my approach at the wedding. And it was always the same song and dance about taking risks with my life.

Whatever.

He could hold a grudge and judge me about my behavior all he wanted.

I had no plans to back down.

I would not apologize for telling those three they had targets on their backs.

Whenever we argued, Elias quickly tossed my words about consequences back in my face. Which, of course, led to fucking. It wasn't make-up sex. There wasn't anything forgiving or sweet about it. Hard and fast, vicious and demanding, and in every torrid way possible.

The fact that every argument led to him filling me with his long, thick cock made me wonder if he picked a fight just to have an excuse to fuck me.

Well, there were a few times all I had to do was scowl at him, and he'd pounce, making me come until I couldn't think straight.

If I didn't know better, I'd assume he wanted me and couldn't get enough of me.

The only explanation was the newness of it all or, perhaps, us succumbing to the heat of our tempers and fucking like rabbits was the only way to calm us down.

On top of it all, my damn traitorous body never resisted him when it knew better.

Shifting, I winced again from the lingering discomfort of my last encounter with Eli.

Marrying him was part of a plan, not to fuck him nonstop.

A wave of guilt hit me.

What were the girls doing? It was strange to be away from them, and it was more challenging to be out of the loop. I couldn't check on the progress of the plan.

Talking to Vik was out of the question. We needed privacy, which wasn't possible with Eli's people always around. Plus, if I shared anything about Eli, it would leave me questioning its rightfulness.

I needed Laya and Cali to talk some sense in me before Eli fucked any little lingering bit out of my head.

Was jumping into this plan the wrong call?

As the eldest, I had to protect them, and it felt like I'd put them in more danger.

This search for revenge was *my* plan.

Fuck. Eli was correct. I had ignited a fire, boasting to those three assholes that I'd enjoy the last laugh. It was uncertain what tricks they had planned.

Vik was there. It was his job to see to Laya and Cali's safety.

But I couldn't shake the new worry that they were now more vulnerable than ever.

The wedding had exposed them to the world, decreeing to Papa's enemies the Vitalis sisters had survived treachery.

The plan was to return to Patras tomorrow and move into Elias's penthouse outside the city center. It was small, a bachelor pad where I had no doubt he'd taken former lovers.

At least it wasn't the Vitalis family home his father had destroyed.

"If you don't pick one of the properties when we return..." he warned as he stalked out of the bathroom, steam trailing after him.

He grabbed clothes set out on a chair without glancing in my direction.

"Then what?" I challenged.

Now, there was another issue we argued about—compromising on a property.

I wanted a home. He had a list of expectations. Neither of us wanted to budge. He had no objection to living close to my sisters, so at least that was a positive in this whole thing.

Who knew house-hunting was so stressful? Or maybe it was only this way with Eli.

Eventually, we'd figure it out or kill each other.

He paused and turned to give me a long once-over, his eyes heating.

My heart skipped a beat, and my nipples beaded.

What am I doing?

"We don't have time for this," he muttered without moving a muscle.

I licked my lips and then swallowed to ease my parched throat. "Then get dressed. I have to shower."

"You shower when I say you shower."

Really? He wanted to go there.

I held his gaze, knowing my following words would set him off. "Your cum is leaking out. I need to clean up."

Something was seriously wrong with me. My desire for Eli never seemed to calm. My ass still tingled from the way his hand had spanked it hard as I rode him earlier.

I couldn't possibly be this addicted.

As he dropped his towel and stalked closer, my blood fired up hot through my veins, and my skin prickled with goosebumps. The predatory gleam in his eyes never failed to turn me on.

"There is no cleaning up for you. You will carry me on you all day long."

Instead of protesting, I rose onto my knees, letting the sheet fall and inviting him closer.

"Is this some animalistic way to mark me, Eli? I'm not someone you can easily claim."

He smirked, and for a brief second, I felt a sensation deep inside me flutter. I pushed it away and focused on the man before me.

As annoying as he could be, there were times like this when I enjoyed his company, sexy banter in the guise of being a jerk and bossing me around.

Maybe that's what it was, a game to pick at each other because we gave as good as we got.

He grabbed my nape, jerking me to him. "You're a pain in the ass, Avra."

"Considering what you've done to me, that statement refers to you." I held his dark gaze.

He shook his head as his lips twitched, and he tried to keep his frown. "Is this how it will be for the rest of our lives? The only way to win in any conflict is to fuck you senseless?"

"Most likely. And what makes you believe I will concede, even then?"

Before I registered what he planned, he took hold of my thigh and flipped me onto my back, coming over me. Gloriously naked and fully aroused, he was everything I never knew I wanted in a lover—dominant and taking none of my shit.

Until Eli, no one had shown me this type of primal lust. It sometimes frightened me, and I couldn't get enough of it at others.

I clutched at his shoulder, attempting to draw him closer, wanting to feel his mouth on mine. Instead, he pushed my legs apart with his knees and nudged the head of his cock at my slick opening.

"Pick a property, Avra. Living in the penthouse is temporary. I want a home."

I furrowed my brow. "You want a home?"

"Yes, a place to start our family. What did you think I wanted?"

"But that checklist?"

"Those are preferences. Something you like will have a majority of them."

I stared up at him. He wanted a home, not just a place to live.

"You make no sense to me, Eli Xenos. I'm not sure I am ever going to figure you out."

"Feeling's mutual." He pushed into me, making me gasp and arch up. "Now it's time to fuck. No more talking."

———

The next afternoon, I went through the City Center of Patras to meet Vik for lunch before Eli picked me up to see one of the houses on my list. The first night in the penthouse had made it clear Eli was the one who wanted to move as soon as possible.

In his eyes, the place was too small for a married couple. Compared to the tiny apartment that Laya, Cali, and I had shared in Prague, Eli's place was a luxurious palace.

But I also understood other reasons for finding a place as soon as possible.

Image.

Living in a home we selected together showed the world

this wasn't an Ozias Xenos-type of marriage with affairs starting before the honeymoon ended, but a real one.

As I approached the restaurant, my security lead, Besa, stepped around me to open my door. Eli's idea of protection and what I'd lived with for over fifteen years were vastly different.

Arguing about it had only led to the typical Eli way of discussion, meaning I was thoroughly fucked and still ended up with a team of no less than six on my security detail wherever I went.

Upon entering, I spotted Vik in a corner where no one could approach from behind, and he had a view of everyone.

Typical Vik.

He rose as I approached, his standard unemotional mask on his face. Until this moment, I hadn't realized how much I missed him.

"He's treating you...well?" he asked.

I nodded and hugged him to throw him off balance. Instead of grumbling, he squeezed me back, opposite to what I intended.

"You did that on purpose," I muttered as I sat.

"I raised you. I know all of your tricks. Be honest—the Xenos men aren't within earshot."

I lifted an eyebrow. "Since our men are mixed in with his, you'd know if Eli wasn't."

My marriage required Vik to increase the units in the area, calling in trusted sources with people available for the work. Many Vitalis soldiers had infiltrated the working ranks of every organization, including Eli's.

"Yes, I hear things." He shook his head, picked up his drink, and took a deep gulp.

Of course, he'd learn about that aspect of my marriage. However, it wasn't his business, and we both knew it.

"We're here to discuss the next step," I stated, wanting no more of that conversation.

Not having to say that twice, he launched right into business. "Marrying into the Xenos family was incredibly smart."

"I told you not to doubt me." I lifted a brow. "We now have access to information that was once completely out of our reach."

In a tone only meant for my ears, he said, "What use is this knowledge if it hinders your ability to make decisions? It isn't my place to make them for you any longer. The orders have to come from you."

"What decisions would you have me make?" I asked in a cool, almost icy way. "It is too soon to move on any of our enemies, and it is foolish to believe otherwise. We are in a wait-and-see period."

Vik pursed his lips and then smirked. Was that a test? Oh, he was good. He wanted to rile me up and see how I'd react.

"Then we continue as we have until you say otherwise."

"Correct." I nodded. "Right now, we only need to draw suspicion about why Eli and I married. We want everyone to wonder what Ozias is planning."

Vik leaned back in his seat. "Then you accomplished your goal. Our men say the other family heads don't trust Ozias's motives behind your union. Some of them wonder now that your marriage legitimizes his claim to the Vitalis lands, which means he is preparing to extend his reach into their areas."

"Things are working out better than expected." I smiled. "The Vitalis sisters are considered royalty in our world, so claiming one of us gives power, whether we come with land or not."

Vik snorted, then grew serious, his face growing hard. "Making yourselves commodities comes at a price, Avra."

"Meaning?" I set my hand on the table, knowing he saw something I hadn't considered.

Vik would always tell me the truth without filters.

"The vultures are circling. You said it yourself, claiming one of you gives power. It's much clearer to me that Laya and Cali are vulnerable. The Vitalis name represents money, land, and legacy. You gave it to Ozias through Eli. Others will try to follow his example."

Goosebumps prickled my skin. "Eli has repeatedly brought this to my attention."

"Explain." Vik's command was more father than adviser. "Since when have you trusted your husband?"

"He doesn't know anything about our objectives. It's more about safety. He believes confronting Caras, Bella, and Korba at our wedding wasn't the wisest of actions."

"In other words, it has caused some friction between you."

That was an understatement. It got me fucked every time it came up.

Instead of answering his statement, I said, "After considering things, I agree with his assessment. Confronting the three at the wedding may have brought attention to Laya and Cali."

"Perhaps, but I watched everyone after you left. Ozias garners loyalty only so far. It is one of circumstance and protection, not a true bond of brothers."

"Getting Laya and Cali into the right families is key. We need ones with power and affluence. They will protect them and become allies."

"Laya is next," Vik said, "and I've identified three major players who are interested in a match with her. I think only one of them is worth the time."

"You work fast."

He nodded, tapping his fingers on the tabletop. "He has enormous power here and connections with the northern Italians."

Perfect, I immediately decided.

"He's the one."

Marrying someone tied to the Italian mafia would be a game-changer, bringing another level of allies and influence. The northern Italians disliked many Greek syndicate heads and questioned their stance on loyalty, especially after what had happened to Papa.

"Your distant cousin Milla married into one of the families," he reminded me. "She married the syndicate boss of a large territory with significant power. The candidate I have in mind for Laya is a close relative of that husband."

"What's his name?"

Vik didn't hesitate, prepared as ever. "Nikolas Galanis."

Knowing Laya wouldn't question my decision, I said, "Consider it done."

Laya, Cali, and I had made a pact to do this: to marry, use our name and influence to connect ourselves with suitable families, and take back what was ours.

I'd taken the first step by marrying Eli.

A pang of sadness filled me. All we'd had for fifteen years was each other, and now marriage would change it, separate us. We'd create lives with others.

We would survive it. Our bond was too strong.

I shut down those thoughts, accepting this as our future reality. We would sort out the rest once we'd rightfully reclaimed everything those bastards had stolen from us.

Eleven

E^lias

I set a box down in the room I planned to convert into my study and stretched my arms above my head. I couldn't express my relief at finding a suitable property for Avra and me. The fact the purchase went smoothly was a bonus.

We had to move the remainder of Avra's things from Prague, which she had tucked away in a storage facility, and some of my furniture from Ozias's estate.

That first night in the penthouse had made it abundantly clear that it wasn't acceptable for my wife, no matter what Avra said. In her eyes, it was ten times the luxury of the apartment she'd shared with her sisters in Prague.

However, we had no privacy. It wasn't possible to rage-fuck my wife in a building full of people. That woman knew the exact words to say to set me off.

And the very idea of bringing Avra back "home" to the estate was out of the question. Outside of not wanting her anywhere near Ozias, the cruelty of pushing her into memories of her loss wasn't something I'd ever entertain.

The mere idea of anyone causing her hurt or distress set off a primal part of me to maim and kill.

I ran a hand through my hair and gripped the back of my neck.

It was maddening to feel so possessive and protective over a woman.

Maybe it was because Ozias had killed her mother, and I refused to subject her to a vile, despicable bastard.

Plus, I couldn't chance leaving her alone with him, considering her performance at our wedding.

If my father deemed her a threat, it would be all too easy for him to slaughter her right in the home he'd stolen from her.

I couldn't fathom the thought of losing Avra. We'd only just met.

We were beginning to understand each other. Still, it would be a long journey before I'd trust Avra. She had her agenda as I had mine.

She legitimized my hold of the Vitalis lands. Then again, they were hers and eventually our children's.

That specifically was the one thing I could count on her to protect.

Our future.

Given the opportunity, she'd kill Ozias but wouldn't destroy the Xenos empire.

It was part of her master plan.

I couldn't help but smirk.

Two predators under one roof—no wonder we fought and fucked so much.

For forty years, I'd resisted the idea of settling down. Now that I'd married Avra, I had no regrets.

"Where should we put these?" one of my soldiers asked as a group of them carried in crates.

I pointed to a corner near my desk. "Over there."

After they finished, they waited for orders.

"Go help Avra," I ordered, then asked, "Where is she?"

"Last I saw, she was in the kitchen, unpacking some boxes."

I sighed. "Make sure someone helps her with the heavy ones. Even if she protests, do it."

One frowned as if he wasn't sure about following my orders. "We were given strict instructions to stay away until the Vitalis women gave instructions to come in."

For the love of all that was holy. Avra had my own people scared of her. Why the fuck had I agreed to a house close enough for her sisters to visit every fucking day?

"I'll go down and tell her myself."

They nodded and left.

This morning, we started the process of packing and transporting our things. I half expected Avra to turn her nose up at the idea of handling the chore of moving herself, especially when we had people to take care of the task. But she scowled at the mere suggestion of someone else doing the work. I stepped aside once I saw her particularities regarding packing and labeling appropriately.

This slender, sexy woman was nothing like what I'd expected. She was the furthest thing from a lazy, entitled woman expecting my men to do the dirty work for her.

And that wasn't the only way she surprised me.

Mostly, I couldn't understand my deep, persistent attraction to her. It hadn't faded yet, only increased by the moment.

I'd slept with many beautiful women. I'd dated plenty of socialites. Most of them were calm and understood social nuances and women's roles. And not a single one held my attention the way Avra could.

Her attitude and take-charge nature made conversations much more enjoyable, even if I disagreed with her, which was most of the time. Plus, she possessed a fire and spirit I'd never realized I needed. Only a strong woman who took none of my shit could handle my darkness, and she'd done that since the moment I grabbed her throat at the wedding reception.

It was more than the sex.

Her mind fascinated me. She viewed the world through a lens of action and consequence.

I smirked to myself, thinking how the terms had become more of a sexual reference between us than anything else.

There I went again, thinking of fucking her.

I walked around the boxes and made my way through the house.

The idea of people suffering the consequences of their

actions *was* a fact of life. I was a practitioner of that very concept. Like the man who'd lied—I killed him for his betrayal. Like the soldier who'd hit a woman, he was beaten and punished. That was life.

As I turned a corner, I paused, seeing Avra carry a large box up a back set of stairs leading to the bedroom section of the house.

The chatter from earlier seemed to have quieted, so I could only assume the sisters had taken their leave.

I followed behind her with her completely oblivious to my presence. I needed to teach her to stay more aware of her surroundings.

No, I'd watched in public. Avra possessed a honed sense of everything around her. Here, she allowed her guard to drop because this was her home. She felt safe here.

A disturbing feeling settled in my chest. If I wasn't careful, I'd come to love this wife of mine.

That was a weakness, a vulnerability—the last person to have a place in my heart died.

My mother.

I paused at the doorway as she carried the box into our bedroom. Leaning against the frame, I watched her as she moved about, unaware of me.

What the fuck was I doing?

I rubbed my hand over my face.

She straightened, noticing me.

"Are you bored?"

I lifted one brow. *With you?*

"The other truck isn't here yet," I replied. I didn't owe an explanation, but it wouldn't kill me to admit why I was standing around.

"Want to get some food then? Before they arrive?"

"As in what a normal couple would do?"

She strolled up to me, tipping her head back. "There is nothing normal about us."

The banter we had and this small interaction brought the uneasiness forward.

"That's true. Where do you want to go?"

"I know a place." She gave me a sly grin. "Up for a stroll?"

I offered her my hand. "Let's check out the neighborhood."

An hour later, after a simple but satisfying lunch at a small place that could only be described as a hole in the wall, Avra and I took the same route back to our house.

"I missed seeing this area," she admitted. "It makes me so happy that Anna's is still open. Papa would bring me there when we came into town. It was my special place with him."

I kept walking, letting her talk. Not once while we ate had she mentioned how much that place meant to her.

I wasn't sure why she'd decided to bring me there or share the vulnerable memory.

Was this some game?

Then she continued, "He would tell me the same story of how he met Mama at a bakery near here, and she didn't like him."

A trip down memory lane was probably a bad idea. It might remind her my father had killed her mother.

"Well, that changed."

She smiled. "Not before she tried to run Papa over with a car."

I stopped to look at her, and she nodded. "Mama was learning to drive, and Papa jumped out in front of her, and she says she forgot to brake."

Avra air-quoted the *forgot* part.

"Is that how they fell in love?"

"No. It took Papa another few months. Papa said she hated him until she couldn't help but love him."

Her words seemed to have solidified something between us that I refused to acknowledge.

Instead, I changed the subject. "I'm sure you've explored other favorite spots since you returned?"

She smiled. "Laya and I, yes. Cali, on the other hand, is on a mission to discover the best dance clubs."

I almost gave in to a smile in kind. "She's young and has yet to discover life. We can't expect anything else."

"Laya likes barhopping, even if she thinks I don't know about it." Avra grinned. "Since Laya enjoys my adventures and Cali doesn't complain too much when we make her join us, I let them have fun."

Avra fiercely protected her sisters, but seeing her give this insight into their bond was like learning a secret. I looked forward to learning more about them. Sooner or later, I'd need to find matches for them. As Avra's husband, that responsibility should fall on my shoulders.

"Layana does seem more...athletic than Calista."

"That's an understatement. Laya loves combat training of any type. Cali, not so much, but she does the required practice Vik assigns. We accept Cali for who she is. As long as we add in architecture and take her to the tourist spots, she's a good sport about all the extra walking."

I took a chance, grabbing her hand to hold it. This more straightforward, more basic form of intimacy and affection was harder to get used to than the raw, harder kind of fucking her. As she loosened up and talked more about landmarks and other things she and her sisters enjoyed, holding her hand and reminding her that she was mine felt natural.

"I was in Prague six months ago," I replied when she asked if I cared to travel. "The day after the holiday, I met an associate at a fantastic new restaurant, Gilded."

She turned toward me, eyes wide. Her fingers remained twined within mine as we walked. "Gilded? My sisters and I often went there."

I wondered if we'd visited on the same day, at the same time, probably passing each other without realizing it.

"It seemed like a popular place," I said as I gestured to a shadier path toward our house.

As soon as we changed our route, I noticed a young girl out of the corner of my eye. She was walking by herself. Someone that young, maybe three or four years old, wouldn't be left alone to roam.

My senses prickled. This child shouldn't be here.

Avra continued talking about Prague and the delicacies

she enjoyed there. Then, her tone grew quieter as she took in the state of the little girl farther down the street.

Her fingers flexed in mine when a man approached the child.

"He's not her father. She's afraid of him," Avra whispered. "Do you see her body language?"

I nodded and tugged both of us into the shadows of the building. Whatever this fucker planned, it wouldn't come to fruition.

"Do you know where your mommy is?" he asked.

She shook her head, glancing back toward the small market stall we'd passed.

"I'll help you find her." He reached for her hand, but the girl jerked back.

"I don't like you," she whimpered, trying to run, but the asshole grabbed her again. "I want Mama."

"You will like me once I help you find your mama."

For fuck's sake.

Had he lured her there? Whatever it was, it was apparent he was going to kidnap her.

Rage boiled up. The fucker had just signed his execution order.

I adjusted my stance, ready to sprint into action, except Avra dropped my hand and darted toward the girl and growled in a tone full of fury, "I will kill him before he takes that baby."

"Shit." I chased after her as Avra rushed the man, shoulder-checked him, causing him to stumble, and then swooped down to pick up the girl.

"Give her back," the man shouted as he righted himself and lunged at Avra. "She's mine."

"The hell she is." Avra turned her attention to the child who clung to her tightly. "Do you know this man?"

She shook her head. Tears poured down her plump cheeks as her lips trembled.

"That's— No. I know the girl's mother." The man stood to his full height, towering over Avra and making him larger than I originally thought.

If he laid one hand on my woman, he would beg for death by the time I finished with him.

He tried to intimidate Avra with his large body and reached for the little girl. "She's lying. Give her to me."

"If that were true, she wouldn't fear you," Avra sneered, shifting the child away from him. "You don't know this girl or her mother any more than I do. Leave before it gets you killed."

"The fuck I will." He reared back his fist to strike her.

In that second, my vision blurred into a haze of red. A roaring erupted in my ears, and the only thought pumping through my mind involved destroying that motherfucker.

Avra was mine to cherish, protect, and kill for.

She ducked in time to dodge the blow he tried to land. She lost her balance while avoiding a second swing, and he attempted to snatch the girl from her arms.

With him distracted, I shoved him hard enough to insert myself between the fucker and Avra.

"Take the kid and back up," I ordered, and I had no

doubt that in this situation, she wouldn't argue but would follow my command.

I glared at the bastard who thought to take a child and hurt a woman—my woman. He was a bulky fucker, tall and ripped, easily twice my size. It's good that I trained with some of my men who were just his stature. Working with them had taught me how to deal with jackasses like this one.

"I take it that bitch is yours. I'll teach you the lesson she needs to learn." The shithead charged at me.

With a quick sidestep, I punched him in the stomach.

Fucking hell, he was built like a damn tank.

My knuckles cracked with the impact on his hard torso, but the pain was worth it, hearing the howl he released.

He circled back, his anger now higher than ever and eyes glazed with murderous intent.

Whatever he felt was nothing compared to the volcanic ire I planned to unleash on him in my workroom.

He pivoted, nearly landing a blow to my face. Ducking to avoid his next attempt, I grabbed the fucker's hair, wrenched his head to the side, and punched him in the temple. I repeated the brutal, precise strikes until I forced him down.

The echo of footsteps rang out around me as my men surrounded us. They remained in their positions, knowing to step in only if I signaled.

Now, if it were Avra, they wouldn't hesitate to engage immediately, but they would keep watching with me.

"Who..." The man knelt and brought his hand to his head, where I held him. "Who the fuck do you think you are? Getting in my business and..."

I cut his words off as my grip tightened. "Xenos."

Immediately, the man stilled, and all the resistance in his demeanor left his body.

"Elias Xenos," I replied, my anger growing with every second this piece of shit stayed in Avra's and the little girl's presence. "You disgust me."

I released him, letting him collapse into a heap on the ground. He pushed up with his hands and staggered to his knees as if in prayer and ready to plead for mercy.

Any excuse he gave would only incite my desire to slice his skin from his face right there in the streets as a lesson to others thinking of copying his behavior.

"It was, uh, it was just a miscommunication. A mistake."

My hands shook, ready to follow through with the vision of filling the streets with the music of his screams.

However, with Avra holding the child behind me, it wasn't something I could indulge in.

The little girl hadn't a clue as to the monster I was, but Avra knew. Would she look at me differently now, knowing what I planned to do with this fucker?

"A mistake." I repeated the idiot's words, looking at his pathetic form. "Is that right?"

He nodded like a puppet. "I'm sorry. I'm sorry."

Oh, I'd make sure of that.

I said nothing, only watched as the asshole crawled backward and tried to gain his feet. Avra moved closer to me with the child tucked close to her side. She set a palm on my forearm, and we watched the man stand and run.

I shook out my wrist. That fucker was big.

"Dumbass," I heard Avra say as her fingers tightened on me. "Make it hurt, Eli. Don't let him get away easy. I want him to suffer before you end it. Make him beg for you to end it."

I glanced at my men, who all stared at Avra. I had no doubt every one of them had just fallen in love with her by making that request.

"You can always join me."

She lifted onto tiptoes and whispered, "I'm saving my skills for three others first, then I'll consider joining you in the future."

Immediately I grew hard and wanted to fuck her. My reaction to this woman made no damn sense.

The mood instantly vanished as a woman screamed, "Isabella!"

Her frantic cries prompted the girl to wiggle for freedom from Avra's arms.

"It's okay," Avra cooed. "We will get you to her."

We rushed toward the harried woman, panic etched all over her face, and my men pursued their quarry.

Barely a second before we reached her, the little girl jumped into the lady's arms, screaming, "Mama."

The worried mother's features relaxed into sheer relief as she clutched her child close, and then she lifted her gaze to mine, inclining her head in a gesture of gratitude.

I released a deep breath and said, "At least we don't need to worry about her identity."

TWELVE

The moment Eli and I walked through the doors of the house after our lunch, a different energy surrounded us. It crackled as if pulsing with residual rage for what the asshole had planned and needing to carry out the retribution he deserved, mixed with this sexual undercurrent that felt as if it burned along my skin.

I wasn't sure if it was anticipation or my senses warning me.

The fact that I found the violence Eli displayed a far greater turn-on than gifts or trips should qualify me as demented. Then again, a weak man would never hold my interest, and from the moment I met Eli, I knew he was unlike anyone I had encountered before.

"Let me tend to your hand," I said, not giving him a choice, and moving into the kitchen where I'd placed a medical kit in a drawer.

He followed after me, not saying a word, only watching me. His eyes continued vibrating with the rage and fire of the incident, but the rawness there set my heart racing.

He needed to stop looking at me like that.

First, it confused me, and second, I couldn't go there.

Those types of emotions weren't part of the plan.

This marriage was an arrangement, a joining of two families for dual purposes. Our inability to keep our hands off each other was a bonus.

"Go wash your hands, and then sit there. I'll get everything out."

He followed my direction, remaining silent, but his focus on me grew in intensity.

The lives Eli and I lived teetered on the boundary of right and wrong. Maybe that was why this skewed view of things made what happened thrilling rather than repulsive.

He possessed the strength to harm me, but he preferred fucking me rough and hard. The darkness inside him called to me in a way I never wanted.

This wasn't acceptable. Eli was part of a plan, nothing more.

As an intelligent, capable, independent woman, I needed no man. Then what the fuck was this man doing to my brain cells? To have someone come to my defense the way he had, to have someone want to protect me for once, to take care of me...I...I...

I shook the thought from my mind. I couldn't allow myself any weakness.

Not like this.

Christ, why wasn't he talking? What was going through his mind? He needed to speak so my thoughts wouldn't spiral. And why the fuck was my body reacting to him?

My nipples beaded against the fabric of my lace bra, and an ache ignited deep in my core. Biting my lip, I set the things I needed on the table next to us.

The second he set his palm over mine when I offered him my hand, the volatility of his emotions poured over me. As if he were a ticking time bomb restrained and ready to burst free.

It was taking all my will not to show him how this enraged beast side of him spoke to my libido.

Or he already knew since he could read my body's reactions better than I could.

Slowly, I tended to the wounds on his knuckles and fingers. The more I touched him, the more the arousal coursing through me intensified. My skin burned, and the desire to press my thighs together to gain a small semblance of relief overwhelmed me.

When I neared finishing, Eli closed his hands around mine. "Are you done?"

"Yes." My breath grew unsteady, and my heartbeat raced out of control.

The primal hunger in his gaze should have scared me, except I willingly offered myself to be his prey.

And he knew it.

"Mine." He grabbed hold of my throat and jerked me to him, sealing our mouths together.

My arms came around him of their own volition, and I lost myself in the demand of his lips and tongue. His taste exploded over my senses; he was delicious and addictive as always.

Maybe we should have worried about anyone walking in or scandalizing the staff. Still, the carnal need riding us controlled everything.

Fuck, this man had me dickmatized.

"This doesn't mean anything," I told him, pulling at the buttons of his shirt.

I couldn't allow him to become my weakness.

What the fuck was I saying? He already was. I was doomed.

"Of course. Nothing." Without care for my clothes, he tore the top of my dress, sending buttons and pieces of delicate fabric everywhere, and cupped my breasts through my bra. "I can't ever trust you."

Cool air coasted over my hot skin, adding to the ache for his touch all over my body.

"That's right, and I'll never trust you. I'm only a prize to you. I'm— Oh, God," I gasped as he scored his teeth along the column of my neck and then bit.

Lifting me by the waist, he shoved everything off the

table and set me on the end before ripping the rest of my dress from my body.

His gaze raked me from head to the juncture of my soaked underwear. Never had a lover craved me the way he had. Goosebumps prickled over my skin, and my pussy quivered as more arousal pooled between my legs.

Eli licked his lips, and I couldn't help but whimper, knowing what he planned.

"Do I frighten you, Avra?" He leaned forward, cupped my jaw, and rubbed my lower lip with his thumb.

I shook my head. "No."

"I should. These hands you like so much on you"—he slid his palm down my throat with his mouth licking and sucking as he moved lower—"belong to a killer. I do despicable things and have no plans to stop."

My eyes fluttered shut, lost in the tease of his stubble-covered jaw as it grazed my skin. How he knew just how to seduce me was an enigma I'd never solve. He coaxed out desires and needs I never realized I coveted.

"Good," I murmured, allowing my nails to score over his shoulder. "I prefer you the way you are."

He lifted his head. "Of course you do. Only another predator can satisfy a predator."

"Don't read too much into it, Eli." Pain and longing bloomed in my chest, along with a tiny bit of panic.

"I won't." He jerked my thong off and lowered it while simultaneously positioning me so my dripping pussy aligned with his mouth. "This doesn't mean anything. Isn't this what you like to say?"

Before I could respond, he brought me flush against him, and all coherent thought evaporated from my mind.

"Eli," I cried out and grabbed hold of his hair.

His tongue speared my core, thrusting, licking, tasting, savoring. He feasted on my clit, driving my desire higher and higher.

It was too much and not enough.

Oh God, right there. Everything inside me tightened and trembled. I dug my heels into his back, arching and pushing up.

I couldn't get enough.

"Eli, don't make me wait," I whimpered.

Fuck, what was I doing? I never begged.

"What do you want?" he asked and flicked my clitoral nub, causing me to buck.

"Make me come."

He nipped the inside of my thigh, the sting of it glorious. "Is that an order?"

"Yes."

"Too bad. I don't take orders very well. I give them." He rose, trailing his wet mouth up my torso, letting the stubble on his jaw brush over me as he moved.

When he caged me with an arm on either side of my head, he said, "Ask."

I shook my head. This game we liked to play had new rules, and giving him this guaranteed that he held power over me.

Real marriage or not, we were using each other.

He was the enemy I'd chosen to marry—the enemy

whose father had murdered Mama and orchestrated Papa's slaughter.

"I won't let you come at all unless you ask. I will fuck you and bring you to the point of going over, time and time again, to only leave you hanging."

"You like making me come."

He brought his face a hairsbreadth from mine, our lips so close only the barest shift would seal our mouths.

"I do. However, I can restrain this enjoyment if I get what I want."

"You wouldn't."

"Are you so sure about that?" he rubbed his jaw against my cheek, the abrasion of his trimmed beard as enticing as his wicked mouth. "You picked me, Avra. Now you deal with the consequence."

THIRTEEN

vra

A chill slid down my spine, and I swallowed it to ease my parched throat.

Eli wasn't playing fairly, changing the dynamic of this game with a completely new rulebook.

"Don't do this and make it something it can't be."

Quick as lightning, he clasped onto my throat, bringing his hard, erect body flush to my sopping pussy. I ground my pelvis to his thick, fabric-covered length to give my aching clit the friction it so desperately wanted.

"It already is. Your reaction says it all." He rolled his hips, the torture so cruel and meant to leave me disappointed.

"It only means I like your big cock."

"You never stop challenging me." He jerked me forward as he stepped back, forcing me to stand and making me positive I'd wear his marks on my skin from his rough hold.

Breath unsteady, I licked my lips and then smirked when his attention shifted to my mouth for a fraction of a second.

"Why would I?" I cupped him, squeezing his erection. "It makes you hard."

"Are you saying this is only about your pleasure and not mine?"

I brushed my chest to his, resisting the urge to moan at the feel of his crisp hair rubbing over my erect nipples. "Isn't it obvious?"

"You talk too fucking much." He silenced me with a raw, brutal, bruising kiss.

A growl erupted from deep in my throat, and I slid my tongue alongside his. This was a rough and angry meeting of mouths mixed with a desperation I refused to focus upon.

I snuck my hand past the waistband of his pants and wrapped my fingers around his cock, the need for him growing at a fevered pitch.

This craving was complete insanity—to want a man this much. It shouldn't matter that he liked I wasn't meek or weak. As much as it angered him, it turned him on.

He broke the kiss. Fury lit his black irises. He released my throat and then threaded his fingers into my hair, pushing me to my knees, my face aligned with his crotch.

Goosebumps prickled my skin, and my pussy contracted, flooding with desire and coating the insides of my thighs.

Without a thought, I worked his pants open. His cock

sprang free, a barest centimeter from my lips. A bead of precum wept from the flared head, and my mouth watered.

The urge to lick him, taste him, called to me. Just as I leaned forward and fell to the desire, he jerked my head back, forcing me to look up at him.

"Is that craving you feel right now only for your enjoyment, Avra? Is it only about my cock, and it has nothing to do with me?"

Why wouldn't he leave this alone?

"Don't read too much into this."

"Are you saying any asshole with a big dick can satisfy you?"

"Stop talking and fuck my face." I clenched my jaw, ready to stand up and punch him.

His hold on my hair tightened into a brutal, almost unbearable grip. "Answer me."

"You know the answer, so why ask?" I glowered up at him, holding on to the waistband of his pants to keep my balance.

"Because I want to hear you say it."

I shook my head as a lump grew in the pit of my stomach. "You don't get to take from me and give nothing back. I won't give you that power."

"I already have it." He gripped his thick, hard cock, pumping it from root to tip. "You're my wife. I own you."

"You don't own me. You're using me, for my name, to legitimize what belongs to me."

He nudged my mouth with his dripping erection. "And you're using me."

I had no chance to argue. With one hard, rough shove, he pushed past my lips, forcing me to take him as far as possible.

Tears burned the backs of my eyes as my gag reflex activated. He pulled out, allowing me only the barest moment to breathe before doing it again.

Asshole.

And I was just as much of one because I liked this fucking primal, depraved side of him. I hated that he knew this about me. I hated that he could draw this need out of me. And most of all, I hated that I willingly allowed him to do this to me.

What was wrong with me?

He repeated the steady thrusts into my mouth, growling as he ground his hips against my face.

"Put your fucking hands down."

I obeyed, not realizing my fingers had worked their way up to his cock. The sounds he made as I stroked and touched him heightened my arousal, but he controlled all of this, and my role was to take what he gave me.

I settled my palms against my thighs as he pistoned his hips back and forth, hard and fast.

The ache between my legs grew, and I couldn't help but squirm. My swollen clit throbbed, desperate for attention and relief. I whimpered and then hummed at the first taste of pre-ejaculate on my tongue.

My moans of pleasure seemed to incite a beast in him. "My wife, my little whore."

Even though he was using me as an outlet for his furious lust and to make a point, I couldn't care less.

I loved seeing him lose control.

I slid my fingers between my legs and worked my clit, needing some relief.

"Stop that, or I will tan your ass red."

I wanted to scream at him, tell him to fuck off, and that he couldn't stop me.

As if he read my thoughts, he pushed to the back of my throat and held still, making it so I could barely breathe. "If you want to come, move those fingers."

Even through the tears clouding my vision, I was sure he saw I planned retribution.

He resumed his torture, powered into me, teeth clenched and neck strained as he watched his wet dick slide in and out of my mouth. Keeping my lips wrapped tight on his hard girth, I gazed right back up at him.

"Even if you want to kill me right now, I know how badly you want it like this, Avra."

I tried to shake my head and deny his words, but it wasn't possible, not with his movements restraining me or because we both knew the lie for a lie.

He grew harder and harder, and his movements went erratic. I braced for his orgasm, ready to swallow everything he gave me.

Except he pulled out, breathing in rugged pants and poising his angry hard cock in my face.

"Get the fuck off your knees." He lifted me up and covered my mouth with his.

This wasn't the wild, rough domination I expected but rather a slow exploration. My heart hammered in my chest.

What was he doing? This wasn't him.

He jerked back, a glint entering his eyes, and the corners of his lips curved. He rubbed his thumb over my swollen lips.

"You're the one who believes in actions and consequences. You sold yourself to me, thinking you could control me. Except you're the one trapped. I own you. Your body, your desire, your soul, your heart, all belong to me."

"Your imagination is getting away from you. No one owns me." I shoved at his chest, failing in my attempt to escape his hold.

Instead, he pulled me closer, turning me, pressing my back against his chest, and whispered in my ear, "It's acceptable to admit your plan didn't work."

"You know nothing of my plans."

"That's true. But I know the basics." He walked me forward, pushing me against the table as he grabbed a fistful of my hair and forced me to bend until my face lay flush on the hardwood.

He slid his cock up and down the lips of my sex, then nudged my opening without pushing in. "We married to use each other."

"That's right," I gasped and lifted my ass, hoping to get him to slide in the way I needed. "Nothing more."

"Nothing more," he repeated and slammed into me.

I screamed out Eli's name as the pleasure-filled pain engulfed me. He gave me no chance to regain my breath, setting a relentless pace. The table jerked and shook with the force of his thrusts, and there wasn't anything for me to do but take what he gave me.

I held on to the edge of the wood, loving the feel of him inside me. With each slide, the sensations grew, and my muscles quivered and contracted.

"Right now, you're using me for my cock, and I'm doing the same for your cunt. Isn't that right, Avra?"

"Stop talking and fuck me."

He rolled his hips in a way that hit that spot deep inside me, making me buck and want more.

"More, Eli. More."

He gave me what I wanted, but not enough to send me over. "This is only sex, am I right? An arrangement. Something equivalent to a business deal, nothing else."

He pounded into me. His heavy breathing and grunts added to my arousal.

Why couldn't he let this be just sex?

Making it anything else meant pain and hurt in the long run.

"I want an answer, Avra." His fingers worked their way between me and the table.

He scissored his fingers around my clit, stroking back and forth. A guttural moan erupted from deep in my throat, and I ground my pelvis against his hand.

"Please, I need to come."

"Are you begging?"

I ignored the question and said, "Make me come. I am dying."

"Then tell me if this is only about using each other."

"Why?" I thrashed, the burning in my body overwhelming.

The arousal and throbbing pushed at every part of me. My nipples begged for attention, and my clit hated the teasing of Eli's fingers.

"Because I want you to admit what I already know."

I clenched my eyes tight.

"I won't give you that power over me," I admitted as a sinking feeling settled in the pit of my stomach, as the madness of the desperate need to come prickled my skin.

He pulled out, turned me, and then positioned me on the edge of the table before thrusting back into me.

He gripped my jaw and brought his face to mine until we were nose to nose. "I already have it."

"It isn't fair. You get everything and leave me with nothing."

I regretted my words immediately. Revealing my vulnerability gave Eli more power.

"How so? It's a balanced scale."

A lump formed in my throat as I stared into his eyes. Without realizing I had moved, I held his face in my hands.

"We can never trust each other."

He shook his head. "No, we can't."

In the next second, we sealed our bodies together. The fucking was brutal, untamed, and a complete claiming.

Fourteen

Avra

A week after moving into my house with Eli, I met with my sisters for lunch. It was the perfect opportunity to catch up and converse without worrying about anyone overhearing. There were so many people about when Laya and Cali had visited on move-in day that it had kept the girls from asking the invasive questions they would have bombarded me with if we'd been alone.

Additionally, stepping out of the house enabled Eli to gather with his lieutenants without worrying about a listening device being planted by Ozias in any of the rooms at Ozias's properties.

I smiled at the security team sitting at various tables in

the room. I'd convinced them that blending into the environment made them better protection than standing over my shoulder or against a wall looking scary. Some of them, no matter how hard they tried, couldn't disguise the fact they were personal security. It was the way they held themselves and the "don't fuck with me" vibe they gave off, even in their streetwear. At least they weren't in suits all the time. I counted that as a win—baby steps.

Laya and Cali spotted me the second they entered the restaurant and came directly to me, not caring that the host expected to escort them to my table. The harried look on his face had me smirking.

Nothing stopped my sisters when they were on a mission.

Cali and Laya took their seats and barely lasted a second before one spoke.

"Don't keep me waiting. I need all the details," Laya said as she picked up her water, drinking down half of it. "I want to know the truth about married life."

"From what I saw at the house, you *looked* like it's suiting you very well," Cali hummed with a sparkle in her green eyes. "I'd say the word for it is—satisfied."

"The correct statement is happily fucked." Laya laughed. "Our men gossip as much as any group of old women in a sewing circle."

My cheeks heated. Were they talking about the kitchen incident?

No, the house had been empty. Well, I thought it was, anyway.

"Oooh," Laya teased. "Look at her face. I believe this is the first time I've seen her blush."

I shot her a narrow-eyed glare. But she was right. Things rarely, if ever, embarrassed me.

"My goodness, she's human like the rest of us," Cali joked. "It only took her getting a good fucking for it to happen."

"Seriously, Cali. Enough with the fucks," I whispered, glancing around the area near us. "We're in a restaurant."

"Oh no, the robot is back." Laya clutched her hands to her chest.

"If I didn't love you so much, I'd shoot you."

"But alas—" She gave a dramatic sigh that made me smile. "I'm your baby sister, and you can't help but love me."

"Dumbass," I muttered, shaking my head.

"Wrong, she is more than that," Cali countered.

"Meaning?" Laya frowned.

Cali gave her a bright smile before saying, "You're a dumbass virgin."

"I'm selective." Laya glared at Cali. "Unlike the two of you."

Not taking the bait, Cali said, "A little too much. I cannot believe you rejected that A-lister who asked you out. Wouldn't it be great to say a Hollywood movie star popped your cherry?"

Cali would never forgive Laya for turning down the current super Hollywood heartthrob. He had been filming in Prague and saw Laya coming out of the city's main library.

He approached her as she entered the nearby park to ask her out, and she declined.

Her logic was that since we lived in hiding, any connection to someone notable was bad. Cali, on the other hand, lost her shit. In her eyes, it was a chance to live on the wild side and have an adventure. Laya disagreed.

"Time to get over it, Cali," I said.

"I wouldn't have said no." Cali scrunched her nose along with her mouth into a pout.

"Yes, we know." I rolled my eyes.

"At least no one died because they took my virginity." Her pout turned into a snort.

"No," Laya corrected. "Vik eliminated him because he was assigned to protect her, not fuck her."

I covered my face with my hands. "Seriously, you two. Enough with the fucks."

Under Vik's care, he clarified that we were a commodity and that our virginities were prizes to use against us. He never cared if we had lovers or went out, but the rule was to wait until we were twenty.

Except I decided to seduce my guard at the age of eighteen. It was around the anniversary of the massacre, and the grief of losing my parents had overwhelmed me.

The guard, more than ten years my senior, needed no seduction. He obliged me after one of my sparring sessions with my trainer.

However, we'd barely finished when another guard walked in on us. The rest was chaos and a world of lectures on making better choices.

Maybe the sparring session and then fucking my guard had set me on the path of what I enjoyed with Eli so much.

"You're one to talk." Laya lifted a brow at Cali. "You fell for a pretty face with no skills."

Cali covered her face with her hands. "Don't remind me. What a wasted experience. He couldn't tell the difference between my clit and my bellybutton. His brother made up for it, so I shouldn't complain."

"Seriously, Cali." I couldn't hide my exasperation. "You slept with his twin brother?"

Confusion crossed her face. "I thought you knew. I told Peter his brother sucked as a lover, and he said he'd correct the situation, so I let him."

I gaped at her.

"Stop looking at me like that. It was my first semester of university. You said it yourself. College is the time for experimentation. If guys can have fantasies about twins, why can't I?"

"Except you lived it," Laya interjected. "Okay, enough talk about Cali. You're the one I want to know about."

"I want details," Cali added with too much excitement burning in her not-so-innocent eyes.

I lifted my teacup to my lips. "The two of you are nosy."

"You knew this about us from the time we were little." Laya set her arms on the table, watching me intently.

I cleared my throat, grinning with this easy banter. We'd never shied from talking about sex, but this silly side brought peace to my heart.

"Married life is suiting me well," I summarized almost primly and with a matter-of-fact tone.

Laya snorted. "I'll say."

"There are rumors about him." Cali grew serious. "Gossip from past lovers. He's not too...rough?"

A surge of jealousy prickled through my blood. The last thing I wanted to think about were the women Eli had entertained before me, especially knowing his tastes.

What we had was mine—the mere thought of anyone touching him brought visions of murder to the forefront of my mind.

"His tastes are...umm...particular," I said, unsure how to say it. "Let's say we're a well-suited pair in that department."

Laya leaned in. "In other words, he fucks her hard and she likes it."

"Oh, for the love of all that is holy, will you stop with that word? People will hear you." I glanced to the side and noticed a group of men watching us.

"If someone is eavesdropping, they deserve to be scandalized," Cali stated. "This is a sisters' lunch with no filters."

"I suppose you're right," I assented.

"We promise to keep it to a respectable tone so it doesn't affect your married-lady status." The grin on Laya's lips had me smiling too.

I rolled my eyes. "Eli doesn't care about things like that as long as I don't threaten to kill anyone."

"So that scene at your wedding didn't go over well?" Laya smirked.

Before I could answer, Cali exclaimed, "*Eli?* A nickname already. Don't tell me *you're* getting soft for him."

I'm a puddle of pathetic need where he's concerned.

I cleared my throat, suddenly eager to change the topic.

"How is life in the house without me?" I asked. "Is Vik driving you crazy yet?"

"That wasn't subtle in the least, Avra," Laya stated.

I kept my tone bland. "Neither of you can take a hint."

"You need to be careful. Don't forget who he is," Laya reminded me as her mood grew serious.

"Remember the plan," Cali added.

"As if I can forget. Eli knows I'm using him." The shock on their faces was almost comical. "He isn't stupid. He knew since before the wedding."

"And he still married you?"

"It's a mutually beneficial arrangement."

"Is that all it is?" Cali cocked her head to the side, studying me. "I saw how he watches you. He's extremely protective of you, which also means us."

"I'm not following."

"It annoys Vik to hell and back, but Eli sent a team to our property as additional protection."

I blinked. Why would Eli do that?

Of course, I knew why. My sisters meant everything to me, and I would put my life on the line for them. So, if they were safe, I remained safe.

"At first, the night of your wedding, I was nervous about our return to the house, especially since Vik had to remain behind on the estate," Laya said. "Our family pushed many buttons that day. Cali and I were easy targets for everyone who wanted answers on why we appeared suddenly.

"When Cali and I readied to leave, one of Elias's chief lieutenants informed us his team would join the Vitalis forces to escort us home, and they would remain as additional protection from then on."

Cali shook her head. "Vik was not happy at all, but what could he say to a gesture of protection for Elias's new wife's sisters?"

"Eli steamrolled Vik. That's what he did." I smirked, and then I sobered. "I upset the big players that night and put you in danger."

"Even if you remained quiet, many of them would have questions, and with us alive, it now challenges the legitimacy of the territory division." Laya blew out a deep breath.

"Everything belongs to us. That is a fact." I sat up straighter.

Plus, with the aid of our relatives in America, we'd discovered piles of paperwork filled with forgeries and deception.

It was too bad for all of them. Papa had planned for the succession of property long before their treachery, and no amount of legal maneuvering would work in their favor.

"You do realize, by marrying Elias and the land moving under you legally, you are officially the godmother of the Vitalis Family," Laya said.

Cali added, "Outside of what he gave us upon our births, everything transferred to you the moment Papa died."

My sisters' words sent a shiver down my spine.

"Eli doesn't know the details. And it doesn't matter. It's not about me but about our children. They will have what belongs to them and everything the bastard Ozias possessed."

"When it becomes public knowledge, the target on you will grow larger. You'll become like Papa, a figure to envy and attack." The fear in Cali's voice had me covering her fingers with my own.

"How is it any different than the lives we've lived up until now?" I asked her.

"The three of us survived with the pressure of being Juno Vitalis's daughters daily," Laya stated. "Plus, we hold the legacy of the old-world syndicate in our blood. Not just from Papa's side but more so from Mama."

How could I have overlooked this? She was not only the daughter of a fifth-generation syndicate boss, but she also carried royal blood from her great-grandmother, who was the daughter of an Italian prince.

"There is no denying our value." I turned my focus on the girls. "I'm not the one we need to worry about. It's the two of you. Marrying Eli gives me protection you don't have."

"And taking one of us is a way to grab power." Laya's words came with a tinge of resignation. "I know I'm up next. Give me the details."

A pang of guilt hit me. "Laya, you d—"

"No. You don't get to make all the sacrifices," Laya said, cutting me off. "Tell me about them. I know there are three. I overheard Vik discussing something, but that's all I know."

I nodded. "Three offers came in from prominent families. Vik vetted them."

"Are any of them good enough for Laya?" Cali asked.

I smiled at her choice of words. "Vik wouldn't put anyone on a list of potentials who wasn't worthy of our Laya."

Laya gave a dramatic sigh. "Keep going."

"There is one I find the most promising. He has ties to our cousin, Milla, who married into another large family, and he wields a considerable amount of power here and in Italy."

Laya drew in a long breath, gazing off to the side. "All right."

"Is he old? Eli works for you but not for Laya. She needs someone younger. Seriously, Avra, give her someone younger."

I narrowed my gaze. "Eli is ten years older than I am. How is that old?"

"To me, that's old."

"Are you done? So we can return to my life," Laya said in a bland tone.

I lifted a finger at Cali, daring her to talk. "He is thirty-three, not old."

"Okay, then it's settled. Accept the offer, and we can plan the wedding." Laya's businesslike reaction to this life-changing decision left a lump in my stomach.

The hopeless romantic of our trio deserved to find love and have a life she chose.

"Are we safer now?" Cali asked, moving on from Laya's future.

"We are safer than before," I replied honestly. "There was never a safe life in store for us, even when Papa was alive. We were born as the daughters of a syndicate boss, a powerful one many feared and envied."

"Then...could I look into going back to university now?"

Laya and I exchanged a glance. We were similar: fighters, strong-willed, ready to do business and rule. Cali was the lighthearted one, more open to alternative futures.

"I want to have a 'normal' life now. If that's even possible." She lowered her hands back to the table after using them for air quotes, considering normal was relative in our world.

"Yes," I said.

My quick response caused Laya to lift a brow.

If I could give Cali even a tiny semblance of the youth denied to Laya and myself, I would do it. At nearly twenty, she deserved to go to clubs, make friends, and explore various subjects. By leaving Prague, she'd given up her studies and the youthful adventure she sought so deeply.

Papa would have wanted it for her and all of us. Papa wasn't the traditional type. Whether we chose marriage or university, he would have accepted our choices. Now, I had the opportunity to give at least Cali this.

She deserved it.

I wanted her to spread her wings and enjoy a bit of freedom she had never experienced before.

"Besides," I added with a devious smile, "it's finally time for us to start using that trust."

"Are you serious?" The excitement on Cali's face was

worth it. "I can study architecture or something that isn't business and useful to the family?"

"Do what you want."

"Wait." Cali scrunched her face. "You want to use the trust to fund it? Are you sure? We've only ever pulled money out of it to survive."

"It's time to spend the money to live our lives. We don't need to hide it anymore."

Papa understood the nuances of keeping secrets and hiding assets as a syndicate boss. This included creating trusts for his daughters in Swiss banks. He funneled millions during his time into those accounts, and they had continued to accrue interest over the last fifteen years.

Vik and the American relatives had kept the funds hidden. Now, the accounts held nearly two hundred million Euros. We rarely touched the money, knowing it would trigger suspicion. But now that others knew of our existence, we could do what we wanted.

"Mama and Papa would be proud to see one of us do something with our lives," Laya said, smiling at Cali fondly.

I deadpanned at her. "What, strategizing to take down our enemies and seeking revenge is just some small minor endeavor for you?"

Exasperated, she said, "No. You know it's not. But I want to think that Mama and Papa would have wanted at least one of us to pursue our dreams. Something *not* related to business, politics, and the family."

"I was kidding. I want this for Cali."

Cali's smile lit up the room, making me realize how different she was from Laya and me. At that moment, I made a vow to find her someone who saw her softer side, someone who could protect her but understood she needed gentleness and understanding.

FIFTEEN

E lias

After meeting with my lieutenants, I headed to my father's house. Avra had left earlier for lunch with her sisters. Something made me suspect that she wanted to make herself scarce, thinking I desired privacy while speaking with my men.

If she only understood those thoughts were the furthest thing from my mind. She was my wife. She belonged with me. The Xenos and Vitalis families were tied together. Sooner or later, they had to join forces, whether she liked it or not. However, it wouldn't happen until Ozias was out of the picture.

Until that day, she would remind me that she conducted

her business separately from mine. There was no mingling of anything, whether information-sharing or discussing problems.

Even if I wanted her by my side every minute of every day, I wouldn't force it upon her. Caging someone like her was as stupid as building a box made of wood to contain a fire. She had lived a life of restraint for fifteen years, and nothing would keep her prisoner now. The fact that I wanted to watch her burn things to the ground simultaneously amused and concerned me.

Avra's hard shell hid a vulnerability I only glimpsed when I'd pushed her that one time. For a woman like her, love and loyalty came hand in hand.

Her sisters had it without question. Watching their simple banter on moving day made it clear they shared a bond I would never have known as an only child. With Laya and Cali, Avra allowed her guard to drop.

Would she ever feel that level of comfort with me?

I gritted my teeth, pushing down that petulant train of thought, and shifted the gear on my sports car.

Calm, cool focus was the only way to deal with Ozias.

Whatever he summoned me for would require all my patience. The last time we met like this, he told me I was marrying Avra. I could hardly wait to find out what today's demand involved.

Fucker.

He likely planned to give me orders on the best way to manage the Italians. But then again, my spies in his ranks said he wasn't acting like his usual self. He was more secretive, even with his own men.

It was odd that, until today, he hadn't called or communicated with me on any issue since the wedding a month earlier.

He was up to something. And I planned to find out what it was.

If it involved Avra, he would have another thought coming.

My wife was off-limits.

My wife. I fucking loved the sound of that.

Comparing our first days together with how we seamlessly seemed to have transitioned into this tolerance for the other's extreme personalities made no damn sense. We still argued like we despised each other, but I enjoyed those verbal spars.

She was the first woman who wasn't scared of me or cowed by my temper. I wouldn't lie and say I didn't care for her.

She was my fucking wife. It was my duty to care for and protect her. Maybe my obsessive protectiveness went a little overboard. Still, the damn woman burrowed under my skin and drove me insane with her attitude about her safety.

Remembering the way she'd jumped into that situation with the little girl on our walk without thinking twice still made me want to throttle her and kiss her senselessly. She had intervened and pulled the child out of danger. Her ferocity made it obvious she'd protect our children as viciously.

Fucking hell, a woman I never wanted to marry fit my life

perfectly. This woman who'd seemed so difficult to embrace and allow near, she *fit*. Avra belonged with me despite the antagonism we insisted on.

Her frosty exterior hid passion and fire that only I experienced. It was in the heat of intimacy that her true spirit revealed itself.

To say that what I felt for her went beyond caring was unsettling. I came from Ozias Xenos, and the blood in my veins held no capacity for great emotions.

Then, why the hell had I spent the morning watching her sleep?

Stop thinking of her perfect mouth and serene expression and get your head on straight, asshole.

Fifteen minutes later, I arrived at the Xenos estate with my mask firmly in place. I studied the exterior and held in a sneer.

Over the top. Opulent. Flashy.

Gaudy.

Just for a fucking statement, he'd destroyed the history of the place. At least the architects I'd contacted a few weeks ago assured me restoring the home to its former historic beauty was somewhat possible. With all the extensions and internal changes, nothing could return it to its former classical glory. Still, Avra would get her family home back.

I stepped out of the car and made my way in.

Ozias lived in a grand, ornate, heartless shell. It was nothing like the home I shared with Avra, where, for the first time in my adult life, I felt a sense of comfort and peace every time I walked through the doors.

This fucking estate was so bleak, nothing but an eyesore to draw attention. I'd only ever associate this place with pain and death.

Including my mother's and countless others'.

Luckily, my early childhood was spent in the countryside, away from Ozias and his cruelty. As soon as my mother recovered from childbirth, he shipped Mama and me as far from him as possible to keep a respectable image and enjoy a life of indulgence.

One day, I planned to show Avra the cottage where I'd grown up. It was a fourth the size of this mansion but full of love and laughter. There were no beatings or lectures on weakness. Instead, I learned my lessons through patient hugs and encouragement.

Mama smiled and laughed during those times. Then, the moment I hit my teens, it had all changed. I was big in height and stature for my age and performed well in my athletic events. This news reached Ozias, and he demanded we return to his main property so he could begin my training as his heir.

I'd begged and pleaded not to go. I hated Ozias. Every interaction I'd experienced with him was cruel, but an order was an order, and Mama had to follow them.

I received my first beating the night we'd arrived. According to Ozias, Xenos men never cried or clung to their mothers.

The laughter and joy stopped. I heard Mama cry more than anything else. The light left her eyes, and she hid her love for me to protect me from Ozias's scorn.

My mother kept the knowledge of her illness a secret until it was too late. I was nineteen when she admitted she was in the late stages of kidney failure. My father claimed it had happened suddenly, a late diagnosis, but I knew enough that it was all bullshit. I'd suspected something was wrong with her for years, but Ozias said she was weak and nothing more.

That was when I looked up my birth records and learned the truth. The pregnancy with me destroyed Mama's kidney function, and Ozias knew it. That was the reason he sent us away.

Out of sight and out of mind. He'd waited for her death, even refusing to find her proper treatment so she'd be gone sooner.

Enough.

I shoved down the haunting memories as I reached the floor for my father's office. Losing myself to the anger only caused more problems when dealing with the asshole.

I strode into his office without requesting permission to enter and said, "You summoned."

He grunted, looking me up and down before folding his hands on his desk.

Oh, he wanted to play lord of the manor today.

"How's marriage finding you?"

As if he gives a fuck.

I arched a brow. "Let's cut the bullshit pleasantries and get to the point. What's the issue?"

"You could show some respect."

I gave him no response, causing a crease between his brows.

He continued, "I wanted to discuss the shipments with the Italians."

"What about them? They are going as planned." I knew because my men kept me informed every day.

He smirked, scrunching his face. "Thought you were off honeymooning and fucking your new wife. Too busy to stay in the loop."

I held in my irritation at his vulgar reference to Avra. My protectiveness for her would give the fucker ammunition.

"I'm always working. One of us has to keep operations going," I stated without inflection.

He narrowed his gaze, leaning forward in his chair, and tossed a pen on his desktop. "Well, things would be different if they were willing to work with someone other than you. They're not interested in meeting with me."

"You tried to meet with them?" I couldn't hide my irritation. "Why the hell would you do that? They made it clear I was their point person. Do you want to fuck this deal up?"

The need to strangle him with my bare hands pulsed in my veins. Nearly a year of work would fall down the drain with this idiot's antics.

Ozias snarled as if his anger had any effect on me. "I thought you'd be too busy having your dick sucked by your new wife. I reached out, and they fucking shot my offer to talk down."

One more disrespectful comment about Avra, and father or not, I would punch him in the face.

"Why are you getting involved now? This isn't your negotiation."

He scowled. "I have a right to be involved. Plus, I don't like how they operate. Deals are made based on the level of power structure."

I furrowed my brow, suspicious of his wording.

"Then what are you complaining about? You need to sit back and let me do the work. As with the Italians, the father is the figurehead. The son runs things. Don't fuck with the process."

Ozias gritted his teeth as the jab hit his ego directly.

I waited for him to argue, but he knew he couldn't. All the families in the territory knew the truth. Even his cronies were aware of how things worked with the Xenos Empire.

Ozias sat on his throne because of me. If I walked away, it would all fall.

I intended the jab to burn.

Ozias mumbled something, dropping his glare to his desk. Then, a calculating gleam entered his gaze right before he switched subjects. "Your marriage to Avra puts us in a better position in the hierarchy. Her family's power might have dissipated, but Vitalis's influence didn't just vanish."

I stiffened. What the fuck was Ozias doing? And what the hell did he mean by that? Shifting from the Italians to Avra meant he planned to strike at me somehow.

I saw it in his focus. And the way the hair on the back of my neck prickled, I prepared myself. I held my temper in check, refusing to give him any reactions.

"What do you mean by that statement?" I asked in the

coldest voice I could muster. "Wasn't the plan for me to marry her to legitimize the territories?"

Deep inside, my temper flared, building with it a rage demanding that I stalk up to him and pound my fist into his face until he revealed what the fuck he was up to.

He nodded. "That was part of it."

He continued to watch me, cocking his head to the side.

"And the rest?" I asked, lifting a brow, aiming at boredom but feeling anything but.

A sea of emotions churned inside me, all telling me he aimed to hurt Avra. I saw it in his demeanor and the calculated confidence written all over his face.

I refused to give him the slightest inkling of what Avra meant to me.

He'd used Mama against me. I would kill him before he touched another woman in my life.

He smiled, smug and sure of himself, as he steepled his fingers and pressed them to his lips. "I'll reveal the answer to that at the right time."

You fucking asshole.

"I'm not a figurehead." He narrowed his eyes, daring me to insist that he was. "Even if you believe I am. I'll show you how I'm not."

In the pit of my stomach, dread coiled. I knew that whatever Ozias schemed would cause nothing but trouble. He was greedy to the core. His plans and accomplishments served only himself. Chaos and pain would be waiting for the Xenos family.

All I could hope was that we all survived the aftermath.

Instead of giving him any indication his words had any impact, I asked, "Did you call me here to waste my time? This song and dance is getting old. I have an empire to run at your behest."

"You will learn to show me respect, Elias."

Not bothering to respond, I turned and left his office.

As I reached my car, I glanced back at the house. The bastard's veiled threat toward Avra wouldn't go unnoticed.

She was mine. I protected what was mine.

If he dared to hurt her or her sisters, I would make him pay.

Avra was my future, and Ozias was the past I planned to destroy.

Sixteen

Avra

What was wrong with me? Why was I so anxious for Eli to be home?

After adding the finishing touches to the pots simmering on the stove before me, I adjusted the temperature to low and turned to wash my hands.

My stomach shouldn't be in knots like this. Maybe it was because it was the first time since we married that we had spent more than a few hours apart.

Was I looking forward to spending time with him?

No, that wasn't possible.

Who was I kidding? Somewhere along the way, the man

had grown on me, and now my emotions were all mixed up when it came to him.

Not that my *heart is getting mixed up here.* It couldn't be.

"Just stop," I whispered to myself and shook my head.

I might as well take advantage of this quiet, empty house. I doubted I'd have evenings like this to myself very often.

Inhaling the scents of all the spices in the air, I sighed. Tonight was the first time in a long while that I'd allowed myself the pleasure of escaping into a simple task like cooking. Our lives had been busy with Vik's schooling, so my sisters and I had made it a requirement to gather at least once a week to create our favorite recipes to remember Mama.

This domestic side of myself was only a tribute to my mother, nothing more. I still had an agenda. Marrying Elias was a means to an end, a crucial step to position myself to avenge my family.

Who was I kidding? What I intended it to be and what it had become were two different things.

I was so fucked. Damn Eli and his magic cock.

A pain ignited deep in my heart, knowing my plans for the future could end this thing I'd built with Eli. I wouldn't stop until I'd killed everyone involved in the conspiracy against my family, which meant eliminating Ozias.

I couldn't let him live even if he was Eli's father. The bastard had killed Mama and orchestrated the destruction of my family.

I turned off the burners and poured myself a glass from the decanter of wine I had been aerating on the counter.

Inhaling the bold, rich scent of the Bordeaux, I moved to the sunroom, which overlooked the Gulf of Patras.

Maybe it wouldn't be a deal-breaker.

Warmth, love, and affection were nonexistent between father and son. Based on my few conversations with Eli and my observations from the wedding, Eli detested Ozias.

It wasn't to the level of my extreme hatred, but it was close.

I took a healthy swallow of my wine and hummed to myself. Eli might not object to disposing of his DNA provider after all.

His support would make things much easier, but there was no guarantee.

Dammit, why did I want him by my side so desperately all of a sudden?

Logic said Laya, Cali, and Vik were the only people I could trust. But that stupid part of me desperately wanted to believe Eli would stand by me.

Shit. That lunch had fucked with my mind.

Downing the rest of my glass, I allowed the alcohol to numb my thoughts as I stared out at the waters as the boats came into their docks.

I was thirty years old, hardened, and matured from a long life of loss and fear. I wasn't some green teenager in love with life, my head in the clouds. Why was I allowing my thoughts to overwhelm me like this?

Fuck. I needed another drink. Or maybe I should eat something first, or risk letting the wine have fun with my head.

Moving back into the kitchen, I set the glass on the island and pulled out a plate. It looked as if it would be dinner for one tonight.

I'd barely refilled my wine when the door opened and closed, signaling Elias's return.

I pushed back all the turmoil and attempted to wear my mask of cool indifference. If Eli came here and suspected something wasn't right, he wouldn't ask but demand to know what was happening.

The fact he could read me was a very annoying ability of his.

When he entered the kitchen, his face showed annoyance and something that sent a wave of uneasiness down my spine.

No need to worry about him sensing anything with me when he was a tangle of irritation.

"You cooked?" he asked, but his tone showed no real interest outside of the fact I was in the kitchen.

I pulled out an additional dish. "Yes. I wanted to make something from my childhood. So I gave the chef the night off."

He nodded and headed toward the stairwell leading to our room. "Give me five minutes."

Well, okay then.

When he returned, there was this look in his eyes that had me worried. I couldn't tell if he was upset or angry.

"What's wrong?"

He exhaled long, taking a bottle of water from the fridge. After he drank half of it, he capped the container and shook his head. "Meetings."

"That's not vague."

He grunted, peeking around me as though to guess what I was making. "What is that?"

"Comfort food."

"And you accuse me of being vague," he muttered.

I poured him a glass of wine and passed it to him. "Did Ozias piss you off?"

"That. And other things." He took it and drank nearly the whole glass before running his hand through his thick hair.

I couldn't help but stare as his shirt clung to the bulge of his biceps with his mindless movements. The man was completely unaware of how his agitation was a complete turn-on.

I bit my lip, tormented with the temptation to push for more. Eli, being so close-lipped and secretive, nudged at some sadistic part of me to poke at him.

"What other things?"

His focus homed in on me, making my heartbeat accelerate. "Why do you want to know?"

"We're a couple. We discuss troubles. Isn't that how it works?"

"Is that what we're doing, Avra? Sharing our troubles?"

"I don't know. You tell me."

"Is this going to be a fair exchange?" His question sliced along my skin, making it clear we were entering more than a negotiation.

"What is it you consider fair, Eli?"

"Let me see." He held my gaze as he crept slowly,

methodically, around the large island as if he were a predator. "I give you information. You give the same. No lies, no evasions, only truth."

"I've never lied to you."

"But you've never given me the whole truth."

"You haven't asked the right questions to garner the answers you seek."

"All of the same can be said in reverse for me."

"Fine. Let's have a question-and-answer session. Brutal honesty is all that is allowed."

The intensity of his presence caused goosebumps to prickle over my skin. "Ask your first question."

"How well do you know them? Are you friends with them, or is it just Ozias? Are you in business with them as well?" I asked.

"Can I assume you're referring to Cristo Caras, Morisi Bella, and Pella Korba?"

I nodded.

He padded closer, coming within arm's reach, his presence a heady sensation on my nerves. My eyes connected with his, and a pulse of lust burned across my skin.

Getting right up into my space, he shot his arms out around me. He dropped his hands to the counter, caging me in, bracketing me.

I gazed into his face as he point-blank put me on the spot.

"Is this an assessment so you can kill them for their part in your father's assassination?"

I lifted my chin slightly, not afraid to answer. "Yes."

"It will cause an uproar. It will destabilize territories."

So, he'd thought of this too. "I don't care." As he narrowed his eyes, I went on. "People need to know they can't go against the Vitalis Family and get away with it."

He pressed his lips together, exhaling through his nose as he looked me up and down. His gaze lingered on me, igniting a spark of desire. Even when I had no right to think about anything but standing my ground, his warm proximity never failed to arouse me.

"Are you officially claiming the status as godmother of the Vitalis Family, Avra?"

I swallowed, hearing that title for the second time today. Just like before, the weight of those words stacked on my conscience.

"I did this before we married, Eli." I allowed my cheek to brush against his as he moved closer.

His hands settled on my hips. "Are you waging war? One target at a time?"

I smirked, loving the proximity of his large body to mine. "You should know the answer to that already. The Vitalis's power remains. Once my plan is complete, no one will forget the price of betrayal. It's all about collecting the pieces to set us back on top."

He narrowed his gaze. "Are you saying that I'm part of the collection? You did marry me to secure the future of the Vitalis legacy, after all."

"I never lied about my motives." I inhaled his crisp scent, allowing my lips to coast over his cheek.

"You never gave me all the details either."

I licked my lips, fueled by this growing thrill of fighting

with him. "I never thought this marriage would amount to more than duty and positioning."

"Are you saying it's more than revenge now?" His expression changed, reacting to my words with an emotion that crossed so quickly that I would've missed it if I hadn't looked at him then.

"How can you ask that after the other night? You already know—" My throat burned, and I turned my face away.

He captured my jaw, forcing me to look up at him. "Know what?"

"This is our children's future. Work with me. We can do this together. I'm going to follow through with this plan no matter what." My voice quivered, stating the truth but not the words I wanted to say.

He squeezed tighter, forcing me to angle my face up. "No evasions, Avra. Those are the rules. Finish the sentence. Know what?"

I drew a quick breath, desperately wanting to keep this part of me locked away. Eli's fingers squeezed, and the pressure there, the show of his craving for dominance, had my pussy waking with need. I pressed my thighs together, trying to stem this instant flare of desire from his fierce grip on me.

"I told you before, I won't let you take everything from me."

He pushed me against the island, his cock pressed thick and hard between us.

"Did you forget I already have it?" he warned lowly. "You orchestrated our marriage. You sold yourself to me. I own you. You belong to me. Everything you are is mine, your body, your soul. Every part of you belongs to me."

I shook my head, which only made his fingers tighten around my throat.

He brought his face right to mine, bringing us nose to nose. "Do you understand what it means to be mine?"

The intensity of his gaze sent a wave of uncertainty down my spine. However, it wasn't because of fear but an emotion I refused to allow myself to feel.

"Don't look at me like that, Eli."

"You're my wife. I can look at you any fucking way I choose."

My lips trembled. "Please don't make decisions about me that you will regret."

If he changed his mind in the future, what would I have left?

"You can't trust me. You said it yourself," I reminded him.

"Look me in the eyes and tell me you believe this."

I tried to turn my head away, but he refused to let me budge, so I could only glower at him. Fucking man had my mind all twisted.

Before I could say anything else, he said, "I have a proposition for you, wife."

"And that is?"

"If I help you complete your plan..." He brought his hot lips closer, brushing them over my mouth. "There is no going back for you."

I frowned, tipping my face back, making sure I understood his words.

His eyes were obsidian pools filled with emotions that sent my heart into a wild, thundering rhythm.

"Are you saying what I believe you're saying?"

He nodded.

"But he's your—"

"I protect what's *mine*," he vowed, sinfully possessively. "There is no escape for you now, Avra."

"I never said I was going anywhere."

He tugged me to him. "I find that acceptable."

SEVENTEEN

Elias

"What do you find acceptable?" Avra asked against my mouth.

I bit her lips, making sure to score the sensitive skin hard enough to sting. "It means there is no going back. You are bound to me, Avra."

She grunted as her hips hit the edge of the counter. She parted her legs enough to fit the hard ridge of my cock against her aching clit and then ground her pelvis to give her the friction she craved.

"Does this mean you're just as tied to me?"

I couldn't hide my growl. "Isn't it fucking obvious?"

Was this woman listening to a word I said?

"Please don't make me regret trusting you," she said as she grabbed my hands and stared up at me with a whirlwind of emotions in her eyes, revealing the vulnerable woman she tried so desperately to hide behind the cold, always-in-control mask.

Bringing her closer to me, I dropped my forehead to hers. "You're mine, Avra. I don't break my word."

She sighed and nodded as if accepting the truth of my statement. Then, in the next second, she threaded her fingers into my hair and fused her mouth to mine.

That was all I needed to surrender to the torrent of lust surging forward. I gripped Avra's dress at the shoulders and shoved it down, forcing her to break her hold on me as I divested her of the cumbersome fabric.

She tore at my clothes with the same desperate need to touch. Our mouths and hands worked with a chaotic urgency to get the other naked. There was no finesse, no gentleness, only a primal lust taking over. Once we were naked, she scored her fingers over my chest, deep and unrelenting, drawing tiny dots of blood.

Her eyes heated, and her pupils dilated, turning her irises into thin rings of green. She kneaded the muscles of my arms, leaned forward, licked the crimson beads along my skin, and then looked up at me with a smirk.

"You'll pay for making me bleed," I warned.

"I have no doubt." She slid her palms around my neck and pressed her body to mine. "You're the one who wants to make me a blood queen."

Holding her tight, I asked, "Am I part of the menu, Avra?"

"Only when you're naked."

I couldn't help but growl as I swept her into my arms and carried her into the family room instead of placing her on the soft cushions of the plush couches. I set her on the edge of the armrest.

"You love playing with fire, don't you?"

"I—it's how we play," she whimpered, arching up against me and tugging me to her with her legs at my waist. "Fuck me."

"Not until you admit you're mine."

"In me, now." A crease formed between her brows, and she tried to reach between us, aiming for my cock, but I grabbed her wrist and pinned it to the base of her back.

"Tell me what I want to hear." I lowered to my knees, leaving her perched on the couch and making it harder for her to achieve her goal.

Goosebumps prickled her skin. "You don't play fair."

"No, if I wasn't playing fair, I'd do this." I plunged two fingers deep into her, scissoring them as I pumped in and out of her while making sure to rub her in the spots to drive her crazy.

"You asshole," she cried out and bucked, only staying on the armrest because I held her in place. "Eli. This isn't right."

"Of course it isn't." I circled her clit with my thumb, and her pussy quivered with tiny spasms. "If you want to come, say it."

She gritted her teeth and squeezed her eyes tight, not

saying anything. She was fucking beautiful, so lost in her torment—her face flushed and tinged with sweat.

"From that first dinner, you knew. That's why you fought me so hard."

"Shut up, Eli. You don't know anything." She shook her head, and then she cried out as I withdrew from her body, leaving her empty. "No, please, don't do this."

I fisted my cock at the base as it screamed at me to slam into her. Fucking bastard wanted to screw her senseless until she accepted reality. But that wasn't the way to get her compliance.

She slid from the sofa, reaching for me, except I moved to face her and tumbled her onto her back with my body caging hers.

She gasped in shallow breaths as a crease formed between her brows and a calculating gleam passed through her emerald eyes.

I smirked and said, "Don't even try it. You're strong, but you can't take me on. Plus, you want my cock in you. You're desperate for it. So punching me defeats the purpose of your goal."

"You're just as desperate." She moved to grab hold of my straining dick, but I captured her hands and pinned them to the sides of her head.

Then using my knees, I forced her thighs apart and positioned the head of my erection between the lips of her dripping sex and to the opening of her pussy.

It took all my will not to plunge deep inside her. She was so fucking wet, and warm, and inviting.

I ran my fingers over her cheek and down her throat while holding her gaze. "Give me what I want, and I will do everything possible to ensure your plan succeeds."

Her lips trembled, and I leaned down to bite them.

"Do we have a deal, Avra?"

I glided my palm lower, along the side of her body to cup her breast, and pinched her puckered nipples. She moaned and then whimpered at the pleasure-filled sting of it.

"I've only had my sisters—"

"Now you have me," I said, cutting her off.

She nodded. "Yes."

That one word sent a surge of adrenaline into me, and I allowed my cock to push in farther but not enough for any form of actual penetration.

"Yes, what? I want you to say it. This way, there is no mistaking what we are discussing."

She lifted her pelvis a fraction. "I'm yours. You have a deal."

"You're fucking right it's a deal." I drove into her with one hard thrust, seating myself to the hilt.

"Eli," she called my name and arched up against me.

Releasing her hands, I threaded my fingers into her hair, angling her head to take her mouth. Our tongues dueled and tasted as I pistoned in and out of her.

I fucked her like a man possessed.

Out of nowhere, her cunt clamped down on me as she rocked into orgasm. She scored my back, tearing my flesh with her nails.

The woman and her fucking need to draw blood.

She pulsed around me, flexing and contracting.

Her moans and mewls rang out like a symphony, and I knew I'd never tire of hearing her lost in need this way.

We'd suffer the aftermath of fucking on the carpet, but I couldn't give a shit, and she seemed to care just as little. Her hips rose with the rhythm of my thrusts as I hammered into her.

"Harder. I need it harder," Avra demanded. "I'm nearly there again."

The sounds of undisguised, wet, untamed sex rang out around us.

And I thought of my men or the staff hearing us for the smallest moment. But the thought evaporated as Avra's pussy quivered around me, making my pace falter.

My body buzzed from the intensity of being inside her, and my muscles shook from holding back my release. I rolled my pelvis, making sure to hit her in that spot she loved so fucking much.

"Oh, Christ," she whimpered. "Do it again, please."

I couldn't help but smile at the possessiveness I felt for her. She only ever begged for me.

Her muscles clenched, and my balls drew up, telling me I wouldn't last much longer.

"You," I gritted out and thrust deep. "Are." My fingers bit into her hips as I speared into her harder and harder. "Mine."

"Yes," she cried out, her back bowing as she plummeted into another orgasm.

She gripped me so tight I could barely move, and there

was no longer any hope of holding back. I came hard, spurting hot streams of cum deep inside her and letting her milk every drop from me.

This was my wife, my whore, my partner in destruction.

She was my family.

If anyone touched a hair on her head, death would be the easiest thing they endured.

Eighteen

Elias

"Everything is prepared as you requested," one of my men informed me as we stood in this tasting warehouse for one of the wineries originally under the Vitalis umbrella but now a Xenos winery.

"Make sure to keep an eye on everyone. I don't trust a single soul here, or Ozias."

After that meeting with my father, we hadn't spoken a word. All of our communications came by email or through our men. On the business side of things, all remained normal. However, Ozias had been visiting our territories in the south, where we held most of our weapons trade stock.

"Reports say he's moved to the southern border line

along the Evros River, near Turkey, and plans to meet with some contacts."

I clenched my teeth. "Send word to the Italians. Inform them the deal is off if they meet with anyone but me."

The lieutenant's eyes widened. "But you've worked on this for nearly two years."

"With Ozias in the mix, it will go down the shithole anyway. If I set the rules, they know I am the one with power and don't like interference. Even from within our organization."

He nodded. "I'll take care of it."

He left, and I focused on the men sitting at the large gathering table in the center of the tasting room.

Cristo Caras, Morisi Bella, Pello Korba.

Fuckers had no idea what was in store for them. I'd let them enjoy my hospitality for now.

Cristo had been the first to reply to my invitation last week for an evening of dinner, wine, and discussions. Then, shortly after, Morisi and Pello agreed to join me. My father's oldest friends loved a good gathering, and visiting one of the most profitable businesses the Xenos family ran was an opportunity they couldn't pass up.

Contrary to Avra's earlier assumptions, I maintained only social pleasantries with anyone connected to Ozias, held no friendships with them, and always exercised caution regarding the complexities of his private ventures. The Xenos enterprises I managed and the one Ozias believed he was in charge of were entirely separate entities.

It was crucial to tread carefully with the three at the table.

I had grown up around them and understood the games they liked to play and the true extent of their loyalty.

Their loyalty only extended as far as the money that flowed in.

Including Ozias, they were all friends, confidants, and co-conspirators. Still, they wouldn't hesitate to throw the other in front of a bullet if it meant they survived.

However, I did not doubt they had all cleared this gathering with Ozias.

My wife was their mutual enemy. And in this case, they would watch out for each other.

They'd behaved so far as it pertained to Avra. However, I expected it to last for only a little longer as they were three bottles into an award-winning bottling of Cabernet.

"Is your business seen to for the evening?" Pello asked.

I nodded as I strolled over to them. "For now. Keeping the Xenos world running isn't something one puts away for an evening. I keep my eyes and ears on everything, day and night."

I took my time reaching them and noticed Morisi and Pello exchange a look before gulping down the contents of their glasses. An attendant, without being asked, refilled the wine while another brought a platter of appetizers.

Morisi took a bite of some bread and then said, "You must have your hands full settling into married life."

"It's better than expected." I took my seat and continued to watch the men.

"I'm sure you're enjoying yourself," Cristo joked,

reaching for some olives. "Teaching that brat a lesson or two..."

Pello cut him off. "She's got quite the mouth on her."

"A mouth better stuffed with—"

"Hey, now." Cristo shoved Morisi's shoulder playfully, mocking a stern reprimand. "That's not right. The boy brought us here for dinner, not to hear you go on about his wife."

I kept my face emotionless, but the fury bubbling up forced me to put the glass in my hand down before I cracked it.

They were playing a game, and I saw through it. They wouldn't get a rise out of me, though. I wouldn't give them the satisfaction.

The enemy of my enemy was my friend. That person just happened to be my wife.

She hated Ozias and these bastards more than I ever could.

Tonight wasn't about me.

I was here for Avra, I reminded myself, to set the scene to help her achieve her goals. And I would.

I tamped down the urge to beat the living shit out of Morisi, wring his neck, and piss on his corpse for even thinking about Avra like that.

It was my job to protect her, defend her.

And I fucking couldn't do any of it at the moment.

This was about her plan, and I wouldn't ruin it.

So, instead, I allowed my voice to go as cold as possible

and take on the tone of the killer everyone knew I was as I asked with a raised brow, *"Boy?"*

Cristo and Morisi guffawed, cracking up with the alcohol they'd indulged in.

"No, you're no boy anymore. I gotta say that much." Pello huffed a lighter laugh, more cautious, not as loose-lipped as those two. "More like you'll have a boy of your own soon."

The thought of Avra rounded out with a child brought forth a fierce possessiveness ten times greater than I could have imagined. She would bear our children and create a future with me. She wouldn't hesitate to protect them as she'd done with that little girl.

None of it could happen until her scheme for revenge ended. A lump formed in my gut. It might be too late.

I stared at the fuckers before me. Getting rid of them was the priority. They posed an immediate danger.

"And she's young enough to give you a son," Cristo added, raising his glass to me.

Of course, he'd want to celebrate a marriage to a young bride. He'd just remarried a wife twenty years his junior to try for an heir.

"Hey, it's not the age." Morisi smirked. "It's how you handle them and fuck them."

He continued with jokes about wives, and Cristo carried on with him.

I clenched my teeth, unable to hide my reaction this time. The two disgusted me.

Morisi's reputation for how he treated his gentle wife was an open secret, a trait he'd shared with Ozias. Mama couldn't produce more children, but Morisi's wife of the last two and a half decades was abused and forced to produce child after child.

Pello remained quiet during this exchange, knowing anything he said would make him look like a hypocrite. A few months ago, his third wife died during a territorial battle along with his two children. Instead of showing respect and mourning, he was hunting for a young bride to bear him more children.

Once their laughter died down and Morisi and Christo ran out of lewd jokes, Pello shifted the conversation, having noticed my reaction to his friends' behavior.

At this point, I wanted the fuckers to know they repulsed me, and I was the asshole who enjoyed torturing a shithead or two.

"I heard you are tight with a few of the families in northern Italy. I don't recall seeing any of their representatives at your wedding," Pello commented.

I arched my brow. "You didn't?"

"Not the northern Italians," Cristo added, nodding at his friend. "Your father mentioned you'd allied with them."

Nosy, as always. They couldn't get anything out of Ozias since he was clueless, so they wanted to pump me for information.

They wanted to know about the connections I'd built. That knowledge brought with it contacts for moving our products, something they had no access to.

"It's true," I stated. "We have an alliance as well as a business agreement. One has nothing to do with the other. We prefer to keep business apart from personal arrangements."

"What did you do to gain their interest?" Morisi scowled and then downed another serving of wine, which a server refreshed. "Who approached whom? Ozias tried to meet with them for years. Even my connections gained no interest."

"I can't get a meeting with them no matter where and what I suggest," Pello added.

I shook my head. *Of course, you haven't had luck.* These idiots employed the same high-handed tactics Ozias used. They couldn't understand that a new generation of power players had taken over, and their methods of one-upping and feather-fluffing worked against them. In an age of technology, facts showed power and the ability to prove one possessed the power they claimed to have.

"It's all about how you approach them and what we can offer each other. It has to benefit both parties."

"Well, no shit, Elias," Cristo scoffed. "You think we don't know that?"

I know *you don't.* They were too selfish and greedy ever to compromise or come down and level in an alliance. This all worked in a give-and-take method. We were all power players in our territories, and as allies, we garnered more influence and strength.

The process wasn't about swinging our dicks around to see whose was bigger.

"Don't think you're the head of the family, *kid*," Morisi taunted. "Marriage doesn't change anything. Your father's still in charge. You work for him, and the deals you make with those fuckers belong to him."

I nodded, listening to the drunk bastard rant. His opinion, or those of the other two at the table, mattered little. They were all dead men walking.

As if I'd cued them, Avra and Laya stepped out from the shadows of a covered patio overlooking the vineyard. Calista had decided to stay behind. She understood the way of our world and trained like her sisters but also accepted she wasn't built like them and preferred books to guns.

Avra's and Laya's expressions showed the calm and cool confidence of two women on a mission. Their steps were measured, not rushed, as if taking in the scene before they confronted their enemies. They moved without making a sound—not a click of heels, no rustle of the fabric from their clothes. Vik had done his duty by Juno and trained these sisters well.

Vitalis and Xenos soldiers trailed in after them. The men I selected to join them were loyal only to me and would die before betraying me to Ozias. They'd lived through both of our leaderships and preferred my way of running things. I treated them with respect and had garnered theirs in return.

My beautiful wife's gaze locked with mine as she approached, and her expression changed for a moment, softening. She wore something I could only describe as form-fitting black and blue combat fatigues. They were fucking sexy as hell and hugged her in all the right places. Then add in the guns strapped to her waist, and all I wanted to do was screw her senseless.

As if reading my thoughts, she rolled her eyes before donning her mask of all-business again.

"Good evening, gentlemen," Avra said as she approached, capturing their attention.

Immediately, the lewd jokes, laughter, and the easy air of camaraderie died. The men stared, speechless and confused.

Laya's lips quirked at the corners as she lifted her arms parallel to the floor, guns in both hands.

"What the fuck is this?" Cristo scooted his chair back but remained seated, glowering at the sisters, and then turned to me. "What the hell are you about, Elias?"

"Are you out of your mind letting her come in here like this?" Morisi shouted.

I shrugged my shoulders. "Possibly."

"Son of a bitch, Elias set up a fucking ambush." Pello shot to his feet, which had the other two following.

Panic and anger wafted from them through their movements and expressions.

I couldn't help but chuckle at their outrage and stumbling. They were starring in a comedy routine as three bumbling drunk idiots.

"I can't believe you'd betray us this way," Cristo yelled. "Where is your loyalty?"

"With my wife." I moved backward and crossed my arms, ready to watch the show. "My future comes first."

"And *this* is how you see it going? You want a *Vitalis* for the future?" Morisi shouted, spittle flying from his mouth.

"Absolutely. Vitalis blood will run through my children's veins. Why wouldn't I secure all the Vitalis land for them?" I tilted my head to the side, seeing the realization fully dawn in their eyes.

They knew.

They weren't that stupid. They had plans of their own.

"Your true problem in this isn't Ozias. Am I correct?" Avra's voice grew hard. "It's Elias. Our marriage and the child we will create."

For a split second, I wasn't sure what the hell she was talking about.

Then it dawned on me, and the surprise on their faces confirmed it.

Avra and I would need to discuss her keeping secrets, especially when someone took a hit out on me.

My entire life, no one outside my mother had ever wanted to protect or defend me. The rage emanating from Avra was almost palpable.

"Wait, or do it now?" Laya asked.

"Wait. I want these fools to know the Danoes declined the job opportunity they proposed." Avra shifted, and our men moved with her. "Only idiots forget how vast our family is. We all have different last names. Don't take a hit out on someone's family."

Sweat slid down Morisi's face, and he knew his time was up.

"Your estates are now under Vitalis and Xenos control. Everything you own, not just Vitalis lands, now belongs to me and my sisters."

"Elias, how can you stand there?" Cristo growled. "You want a future of letting this bitch call the shots?"

My temper flared. Holding back as one of them disrespected my woman time and time again was over.

Maybe it was the look in my eyes or something else. Cristo reached for the gun at his waist. I ducked, and Laya redirected her aim, shooting off one bullet and hitting Cristo between the eyes.

My relief lasted barely a second before chaos erupted. Morisi and Pello jumped into action, pulling their guns alongside all our men.

Everyone's soldiers, including the three fuckers', were trained to stand by and wait for a signal, never to interfere with their bosses. Still, now, all bets were off the table. The Caras, Bella, and Korba men split up, attacking the Xenos and Vitalis forces.

I searched for Avra. I didn't give a fuck about anyone else. I dodged a punch to the face and socked an asshole in the gut as I weaved my way around to the area where I had last seen Avra.

That's when Morisi appeared and charged right at me.

"Let's go, motherfucker." I welcomed the chance to unleash my fury for all the barbs he had spilled against my Avra.

We were similar in build and the closest in age—he was in his late forties, and I was just turning forty. And the fact he trained similarly to me meant we were an even match, and I couldn't let my guard down, no matter that he was drunk. Actually, I should keep it up more since there was no telling what he'd do.

Right as he reached me, I knocked him hard in the face, sending him a few steps back. "You deserve this and more."

"You do all this for pussy." He spit out blood, his face a play of outrage. "She's a whore, everyone knows this. Ask anyone in Prague."

We threw punches, bobbing and weaving, and the need to destroy him blinded my vision. The craving for violence-filled retribution fed my blood as it pumped through my veins.

I shook off the few hits that he landed, but eventually, I grabbed him by the hair and brought him onto his knees, pummeling his head.

"You don't deserve the right to look at my wife. To think of her." I jerked his head back and started my retribution on his face.

He scraped and clawed at my arm, trying to breathe.

"You didn't listen when she told you she'd have the last laugh…" I shifted my hold, gripping his head differently. "She spoke the truth, and now you pay."

I twisted my hands in opposing directions, and the snap and crackle of bones echoed out as I broke his neck. Throwing the fucker to the floor, I stared at my blood-soaked, swollen hands and blew out a deep breath.

He deserved everything he got. Technically, this was Avra's kill, but I was in no mood to wait for her to take care of this.

I took inventory of the area around me. Bodies were scattered throughout the area, but there was no sign of Avra.

My heart hammered in my chest.

Where the fuck was she?

Yes, I knew she could hold her own. But this wasn't the world she'd grown up in, no matter how well Vik had trained her.

She was my fucking future, and I'd protect her whether she liked it or not.

I homed in on Cristo's slumped body.

Laya had taken care of that jackass.

With Cristo and Morisi out of the way, it was time to find Pello.

I heard her before I saw her. "I'm not letting you get away, you fucking coward."

Running toward the voice, I found her chasing after Pello and being intercepted by one of his soldiers, who grabbed her by the waist.

Immediately, a red haze coated my sight, and I darted for them. Avra saw me and nodded, instinctively knowing what I had planned. I pulled the gun from my waist as she went limp in the soldier's arms, and he lost his grip on her. I shot, hitting the dick in the face.

"Don't you fucking do that again," I ordered as I helped her up.

Her response was to tug me to her and kiss me.

She pushed me away at the screech of car tires and rushed toward the lawn leading to the parking area. "I won't let him escape. I can't."

I chased after her, arriving in time to see Avra skid to a stop and raise her gun. She aimed it at Pello while he pointed his at her.

My heart stopped, and all the air in my lungs froze. I was too far away to reach, help her, or block her. I opened my mouth to shout, but I held it back, not wanting to distract her.

My life spun in slow motion, except my limbs remained stuck in place. Watching them square off, the idea of him killing her, the thought of losing her.

The twin blasts jarred me out of my paralysis of seconds earlier, and a manic rage engulfed me. If anything happened to her, the world would learn the true nature of the monster I was.

I tore across the path, then jerked to a stop, unable to comprehend what I saw.

Pello lay in a crumpled heap on the grassy field. Avra stood a short distance from him, stock-still as if in a daze. After a few moments, she staggered and ran in Pello's direction.

I rushed to her, not trusting that Pello was indeed down. We reached him at the same time. I fought to catch my breath.

Avra remained stoic, unflinching, as I wrapped my arms around her.

Blood spilled from the single hole in the center of his forehead. He gasped for air, each inhale growing slower and slower.

A warm stickiness coated my fingers, and I glanced down to find the sleeve of Avra's suit shredded and blood seeping from her arm.

"You're hurt." I lifted her arm to inspect the damage.

She twisted, trying to take a look. "It's not so bad. He's a lousy shot."

"You're fucking out of your mind. You could have died."

She clenched her jaw. "He couldn't go free."

"I would have found him for you." I jerked her to me, my irritation growing by the second. "Your life is my priority."

"And your life is mine." She poked me in the chest. "Got it? He is the one behind the hit."

"Yes, the hit. When did you find out?"

"This morning."

"And you didn't think telling me before this meeting was important?"

"You protect me. I protect you. That's the deal."

I leaned in, narrowing my gaze. "The terms are very clear. You are mine. You belong to me. In exchange, I help you serve up your wrath."

"Then help me serve it, husband. They targeted my family. This includes you."

NINETEEN

A week after what I liked to call the elimination at the vineyard, I waited for Cali outside a new modern art gallery. She insisted that I would surely find a piece that Eli and I could agree on for the dining room.

I doubted her optimism. However, Eli and I had decided to meet here after he finished his business with his chiefs.

My phone buzzed with a text from Cali.

Cali: I am running late. Be there in a few minutes.

"A few," I muttered and shook my head.

In Cali terms, that could mean anywhere between five and fifty. I might as well check out the pieces on my own for a "few" minutes.

I smiled to myself as I approached the door to the gallery and then frowned as my security lead, Besa, pushed open the door.

"I can go in without assistance. Eli is going overboard with this."

Besa shrugged. "We have our orders. He doesn't want you straining your arm until the doctor says you have completely recovered."

"It's a door. This is annoying."

No matter what Eli believed, my arm worked perfectly well, and outside of healing skin, there was nothing amiss. An occasional muscle twitch was part of the process of things knitting together. It wasn't as if the bullet hit anything vital.

Pello had barely grazed my arm. The idiot needed glasses. He shot like stormtroopers used their blasters—everywhere but at the target.

My phone dinged again.

Eli: Stop giving Besa a hard time.

Me: I know he didn't rat on me. He's a Vitalis. How do you know I did anything to him?

Eli: I know you. And let me correct you. Besa is a Xenos with Vitalis ties.

The hell he was.

Eli: Stay calm. We can fight and fuck about it later.

Me: I hate you.

Eli: Do you?

I sighed. What I felt for Eli was nowhere in the vicinity of hate.

Me: No.

Eli: That's what I thought.

Me: Finish up and come find me so we can argue about the proper aesthetics for our dining room.

Eli: I'll be there shortly.

I tucked my mobile back in my handbag and strolled through the blown glass section. I came across a beautiful piece resembling flowers at one angle and ocean waves at another. It was perfect for Eli's office.

What the fuck was I doing?

Was I looking at art for a home I shared with a husband?

Me. Avra Maria Vitalis.

How was this my reality?

And why wasn't I upset about it?

If it had stayed mind-consuming, livewire attraction and sex, I wouldn't have accepted Eli into my circle as my family.

There were genuine emotions between us, a strong connection. We trusted each other in a way I never thought possible. I wasn't sure when it had happened or precisely why. He was the only one, aside from my sisters and Vik, who knew how we maintained the Vitalis fortune and continued to grow the family influence. It felt natural to share with him, and he reciprocated in kind. We even discussed future plans for managing the territories, details that I'd never shared with anyone, not even Vik or my sisters.

We'd become a partnership, and I knew without a doubt that he would never betray me. We fought still, but in unimportant ways that would always happen when two headstrong people butted heads.

I touched the brilliantly colored glass and pulled my fingers away, almost as if it had burned me.

I felt the emotions in the piece and would buy it.

The fire that created this sculpture burned hot and frightening, exactly the same way my emotions whirled inside me. They were too big, too heavy, molten, and I feared naming them.

Was it too soon? Could I really feel this much? What was happening to me? For the first time in my life, something intimidated me.

I pushed those thoughts back, blinking a few times.

I had to snap out of this. Cali would notice my mood in an instant, and so would Eli. Those two had a way of reading me when no others could.

I blew out a deep breath and glanced around me. Besa nodded as he kept a discreet distance in the background, pretending to admire a painting.

No, something wasn't right. A prickling sensation skittered along the back of my neck like eyes other than my security's were on me.

Knowing never to question my instincts, I took a path closer to Besa and his men. I paused in front of a bicycle shaped out of old spoons. It was whimsical and amusing.

At the same time, a woman approached to study the piece. I'd noticed her earlier in passing but thought nothing of it. She tilted her head side to side and expelled little sighs and murmurs as though she were some great art critic.

God, if only Cali was here. She wouldn't keep her mouth shut about this one. Our experiences with "art connoisseurs" in Prague were too many to count. We'd turned it into a game to pick out those who truly enjoyed art versus the fakers.

Go ahead, lady. The piece isn't something I'd buy. I'll stick to the glass.

I barely finished my snarky thought when she moved closer, stepping too near for comfort. Besa shifted as if to intervene, but I shook my head.

I couldn't be in danger *here*, in public, in the daylight. Even if I were, I could handle it.

Deciding to be just as rude, I stared at her, taking her in, giving her my, as Laya called it, "bitch face."

If she wanted something from me, she should come out and say so. I turned, facing her without changing my expression. At first glance, something seemed familiar about her, but no name or specific memory came to mind.

She was a natural beauty, years younger than me, closer to Laya's age, with long glossy locks of a light chestnut. She wore a tailored black jumpsuit, accentuating a curvy, toned body. Her eyes were nearly black and held no kindness or feeling.

It was apparent she didn't like me.

Something about her looked familiar. Perhaps I'd passed her in town, but nothing came to me. I couldn't place her.

"I'm Francesca," she stated as if I should know her.

Was she a local celebrity? Cali may know, or Laya.

When I gave her no reaction other than a head nod, a flash of irritation crossed her face before she schooled it away.

"Isn't it a lovely design?" she asked, annoyed. She

gestured at the artwork, and I nodded again. "Such a master-piece. All that blue. The incorporation of those tones with the theme..."

The theme of what? It is a fucking bike made out of spoons sitting on a blue tablecloth. What the hell are you talking about?

I remained quiet, letting her ramble about the piece. None of what she said matched the description provided by the artist, an environmentalist aiming to highlight the waste humans leave behind in the world.

After a few minutes, she asked, "I'm sorry, what was your name again?"

"I didn't say." I glanced at her. "Then again, you already know it."

A crease formed between her perfectly arched brows. "You shouldn't have come back."

"Do I know you?" I asked in a tone one used with an errant child. "Did we meet in a different life? Let me guess, we weren't friends."

"The Vitalis name died fifteen years ago and needs to stay that way." The venom in her words made me wonder if her hatred came from last week's elimination.

"It never died. It's time to relearn local history." I kept my face an emotionless mask, and my focus trained on her.

The best way to poke at an unhinged being was to get them to act the fool.

She jabbed her finger at my face. "Mark my words, you and your sisters will regret returning."

Fire burned under my skin, molten and ready to scorch.

She could threaten me all she wanted, but not my sisters. I'd do it if it meant buying every piece in this gallery as I destroyed that pretty face.

The muscles in my hands quivered, ready to grab her hair and smash it into the masterpiece of blue.

"Listen, Francesca. Word to the wise. Stay out of matters that don't concern you," I warned. "I'm one enemy you can't afford to make."

"It *does* concern me." She put her face in my space, clenching her teeth. "Elias is an idiot to downgrade to a woman like you."

Downgrade?

Definitely a former lover. All of this because he left her?

"Meaning?" I ordered.

"Exactly what I said. You have a name tied to an old family, nothing more. The influence and connections it had are long gone. You're old, worn out, and unremarkable. Walking away from the power I brought was a huge mistake."

Well now.

Vik had mentioned lovers, and considering I wasn't an innocent, I couldn't care less about who Eli had banged in the past.

Yes, Eli knew how to fuck the hell out of a woman and leave her begging for more, but this level of crazy? Eli sure knew how to pick them.

What the hell was I talking about? According to Cali and Laya, my past choices weren't much better.

I studied Francesca, giving her no reaction to the barbs.

People like her hated when the targets of their ire refused to engage.

She fidgeted, and her face flushed. That's when I remembered where I'd seen her before—at my wedding. I hadn't taken much notice outside of the fact Cali had pointed out a brunette who scowled at me every time she glanced in my direction.

Everyone's eyes were on me and my sisters that day, so curious and dirty looks were par for the course.

"Used up," she repeated. "Elias will tire of you."

I sighed. Eli's stance on fidelity was well-known. There wasn't a single speck in my soul that believed he'd cheat on me. Plus, he knew I'd cut his dick off if he thought about it.

"He'll lose interest. I promise you. He'll want someone young. Someone fun."

I wanted to say it was the fact she was young and couldn't see this was a losing fight, a one-sided one at best, but there had to be more. But honestly, I was over it.

Pursing my lips, I said, "Are you done? This tantrum is boring."

Turning, I nodded to Besa and walked toward the front of the gallery.

"You don't believe me?" She hurried after me. "I know him. I know how to please him. I know how to drive him crazy and make him come back for more."

Cali would get an earful for standing me up and making me endure this insanity.

And where the fuck was Eli? I'd rather he handle this fucked-up twat.

I continued to ignore her as I stepped out onto the street. Besa blocked Francesca's way.

"Stand back," Besa ordered as two other guards positioned around me. "You need to leave Mrs. Xenos alone."

"I'm only speaking the truth."

A headache began to brew at my temples, and I stared at my waiting car. I thought of something Vik had said before we left Prague.

"Your enemies come as men and women. Never forget this. Be prepared to exact your power wherever necessary. Sometimes, it's in private, and at others, you will make a public lesson of them."

My hands shook. It was time to shut this gasbag down.

I returned to where the three men blocked Francesca from following me. "Step aside, gentlemen."

None of them moved.

"Xenos will discipline us if anything happens to you," Besa stated.

"Get out of my way."

Reluctantly, they all moved but stayed nearby.

"Look, Francesca. I have nothing against you, so I suggest you leave me alone. I'm giving you this second and last warning. Your loud display does you no service. It makes you look desperate. You are above this. Get yourself together."

She clenched her jaw. "I'm not a child. Don't talk to me like one. Your name doesn't give you power in this city. All Vitalis are scum."

And my patience with this brat was over.

"You know my family name and background enough to

call me scum. That's power in itself. In contrast, I don't know or care to know yours. You are nothing to me and less to my husband. Come near me again, and I will retaliate."

Fucking hell.

I dismissed the altercation and pivoted to walk away. Before I could get far, a piercing scream echoed out, and a body hit me from behind, knocking me down. Francesca grabbed my throat. I shifted to the side, fast enough to break her grip.

With my elbow, I clocked her on the side of the head and then clutched her neck in the way she had attempted to get mine. I shoved her to the ground, squeezing her airway, and held her in place with my knee on her chest.

"Attacking anyone when their back is turned makes you the scum. I can kill you with a small twist of my wrist."

Whimpers and moans escaped Francesca's lips, and tears streamed from her eyes, but they still blazed with hatred.

"I could let you live. Show Vitalis mercy if you don't speak of my family again. This includes Elias." I eased my hold and leaned in. "But we know that isn't possible. You've made me your enemy when I don't know you."

She croaked out, "You will die."

"Not before you." Grasping her throat with one hand and the back of her neck with the other, I broke it, giving no fucks that I'd killed someone in public.

"Oh, for fuck's sake. Why would you do that? We were here," Besa said as I stepped away from Francesca's body.

"He's going to kill us." He stared at me with sheer panic, and then the expression on his face changed to fear as he saw

Eli. "I swear it happened within seconds. She does what she wants. You know this."

"Yes, I know. Have it cleaned up as if this never happened. Make sure to wipe all surveillance."

Eli approached, taking my hands in his, and then tilted my neck to examine the marks. He turned his attention to Francesca, sprawled on the sidewalk, and fury lit his gaze.

"I will never allow anyone to threaten or attack me and get away with it again."

He nodded, brushed his lips against my forehead, and touched my head against his chin. "That's what a blood queen does."

TWENTY

E^{lias}

Steam wafted from the hot bath as I held Avra against me. It was near sunset, and a deep golden glow filled the bathroom. I felt an unexplainable need to hold her and keep her close. It burned inside me with no signs of easing since I found her in the aftermath of the altercation with Francesca.

My wife, the woman I planned to spend the rest of my life with, the future mother of my children.

The last place she needed to be was near blood or violence, much less be at the center of it. But that wasn't how it worked with us in our world.

Things like this happened every day.

Except it seemed as if she fucking courted danger more than any other female I had ever encountered.

It wasn't just her bloodline that made her a prime target, but also because she refused to be anyone but herself. There was no taming that temper or sense of purpose.

No matter how much it drove me mad to know she'd engaged in a physical altercation, hearing Besa's version of the events, I knew Avra had given plenty of warning to leave her alone, and then it was Francesca who attacked.

Thank God Avra had trained and knew how to handle herself. According to the soldiers, everything happened so fast that even if they'd intervened, Avra would have been unable to avoid injury.

It would have kept her from killing someone with her bare hands, but she appeared unbothered by it, making it very clear that this wasn't her first time taking a life like that.

Would Avra have received the same unapologetic combat education Vik put his other recruits through? Rumors circulated about Vik's methods at his school, as he liked to call it. They were brutal, even by my standards. To pass into the second level of training, each soldier had to hunt and kill an enemy of the Vitalis family without weapons.

I couldn't imagine what it was like for Avra and her sisters to be raised by one of the most notorious seconds in our world. The man loved the women. It was evident from how he went out of his way to watch over them. But affectionate, he wasn't.

I could never thank him enough for teaching Avra to

react and protect herself with as much force as necessary. If Avra hadn't killed Francesca, I would have found a way to put a bullet between her eyes by the end of the day.

What was Francesca's aim in going after Avra? I'd made my stand on cheating abundantly clear. Showing up to the wedding was an idiot's move, and now she was dead.

"Are you finished brooding? I'm fine. It's time to let it go."

"Letting it go is easier said than done."

"Allow me to entice you then." Avra stretched her arms over her head and exposed her lush breasts above the water.

I cupped them and asked, "Do you realize how much of a pain in the ass you are?"

"I'm sure you're going to tell me." She threaded her fingers behind my head and slid them to my nape as she looked up at me.

"You have security for a reason. Let them do their job."

"Like you did with the man and the little girl?"

I couldn't hide my annoyance. "Those are two different circumstances."

"That's true." She turned, straddled my hips, and caged my shoulders with her arms. "One of your harpies stalked me in a gallery and then attacked me. I sent a message to all who may consider fucking with me in the future."

Guilt bubbled up. It was my job to protect Avra, and I'd failed.

"I'm sorry."

"Why are you apologizing? You weren't there."

"I'm sorry for the situation." I shook my head, slowly rubbing her arms and being careful not to press too hard over her still-healing gunshot wound. "Francesca was my lover before your marriage proposal came to light," I explained, feeling the need to clarify why this had occurred. "I slept with her intermittently for about two years. I made it clear from the beginning that nothing would come of it. I was direct about our relationship being casual. I never promised anything long-term or any commitment."

"Her thinking otherwise isn't your fault. And neither is the altercation."

"You aren't upset about her cornering you at the gallery?"

"No. I would be stupid if I were."

I stared at her, unsure whether to be upset or in awe of her ability to handle a crazy, jealous ex-lover as if it were an everyday thing.

"I saw her at the wedding. No one invited her, just in case you wanted to know. And I made sure she stayed away from you. The last thing a bride wants is to face their husband's ex."

"If you could see your face right now." She laughed, jostling the water with her movement. "You're ten years older than me. I'm well aware you had a life before me. I expected you to have more than a few ex-lovers who hated me for marrying you. I locked it down while they couldn't."

Marrying me was locking it down. She'd come to me with a proposition, and I accepted.

"Are you annoyed that I said I locked it down? Cali says

that is the correct terminology for when a woman gets a ring out of a man who never planned to marry."

This woman was making fun of me. I narrowed my eyes, holding back my need to grab her throat. The marks from the fight were there. I wouldn't think about that now. This wasn't the time for that.

"You think this is funny?"

"Very. You want jealousy, and I'm not giving it to you."

Her attention went to my clenched fist on the rim of the tub, and a crease formed between her brows. She reached over, taking my wrist.

"Open your hand," she ordered.

I followed her direction, and then she lifted it to her neck.

"I'm not fragile. Don't forget, I killed a dumbass bitch today." She smiled.

I rubbed my thumb along her mouth. "We will talk about that at a later time."

"I'm sure we will." She leaned in. "Let's finish this discussion so we can get to the part where you choke me and fuck me. Humm."

"You make no sense." My hold tightened on her. "And you're a pain in the ass."

"Yes. You mentioned this earlier." She pursed her lips, trying to hold in a chuckle. "Are you still confused about why Francesca doesn't bother me?"

"Actually, yes," I answered honestly and then groaned as she adjusted her position.

My cock grew hard along the seam of her pussy as a surge of lust rushed forward.

"Is there a woman somewhere in the world, perhaps a lost lover you can't forget? Be honest."

I tried to focus on her words and not her hot cunt teasing me. Then her question sank in, and outrage cleared my focus.

My fingers flexed on her neck, and I clenched my teeth. "I told you before, I never planned to marry. The only woman I can't get out of my fucking mind is you. Half the time, I wonder if you're starting a war with someone, and the other, I'm counting the minutes until I can plow my cock into your cunt."

I bucked up against her, letting the hard ridge of my dick slide along her heat. She gasped and then ground down on me, wanting more of the friction.

"Then get it through your head." Her voice grew husky. "I don't care about your past because none of them matter to you. The same goes for me. I don't pine over any past lover. You take up too much space in my life."

The thought of anyone having touched her, tasted her, or slid into her had me craving to slice the skin off each of their faces.

"Let me give you a warning." I bit her lower lip hard enough to sting.

Her eyes dilated as goosebumps broke out over her flesh, and her nipples pebbled. Never had anyone responded to me this way. Especially in the mood I was in now, where my blood boiled with fury.

"I'm listening." She pressed her wet chest to mine and

then scored her nails over my shoulders, giving me a taste of the pain I'd just given her.

I fisted her hair with my other hand and jerked her head back.

So fucking beautiful.

She was so tough everywhere else, but she gave me every bit of her control.

Right now, she was at my mercy, so exposed and vulnerable. She trusted me completely, knowing I wouldn't hurt her.

She was fucking mine, no one else's. I resisted the primal drive to mark her with my teeth.

"I'm not like you." I trailed my palm from her neck, over her collarbone, between her breasts, and down her abdomen, continuing the journey until I reached the apex of her sex. "I'm jealous. I'm possessive. I'm overprotective to the point I become unhinged. And the fact I enjoy killing a motherfucker is a bad omen for anyone who ever tasted what belongs to me."

"I'm thirty, Eli. Staying a virgin to this age is rare or a lie." Her lips parted, and her face flushed.

"Logic has no standing when it comes to you." I parted her and thrust two fingers into her swollen cunt as I circled her sensitive clitoral nub. "Never let me meet an ex unless you want it to be the last day of his life."

"That's ridiculous." She threw her head back, eyes closed, riding my hand as I pumped in and out of her.

"Never forget. You chose me. Now, you deal with the consequences."

Water spilled from the tub as her movements grew frantic.

"Actions...umm... Consequence... Oh fuck—Eli."

I sat up, freeing her hair, and encircled my arm around her waist. "Come for me, Avra. Show me how much you love this butcher's hand inside you."

Her orgasm ripped through her cunt, contracting and spasming while I took every bit of her pleasure out of her. I held her up, watching her lose herself in her climax.

As she slowly descended, I leaned her against the edge of the tub seat, spread her thighs, and poised her over my hard, aching cock.

"I like these consequences." Her eyelashes fluttered open, her ordinarily green eyes darker and hazed. "I want more."

"Of course you do. You have a greedy, hungry cunt."

She shifted her pelvis. "Then feed it."

"Like this." I slammed into her, making her scream and grip my shoulders.

I held her still, reveling in her delicious feel. She fit me like a glove, so soft, so warm. She was made for me.

And she had no idea how serious I was about torturing and then killing any past lover of hers I encountered.

I was a killer due to Ozias and his actions.

For Avra, I'd become a monster. She was mine.

I cupped her breast, teasing her nipples, giving her the edge of pain she loved.

She moaned, biting her lip and rocking against me.

"Tsk, tsk." I slapped her beautiful ass, which made her

clench around me. "If you want to come again, then you use my cock and earn it. No cheating."

She lifted a brow. "As if you can sit there and let me do all the work. You wouldn't last more than a minute."

"Is that a challenge?" I asked, setting my hands on her hips.

She positioned her knees on either side of me and slid up and down at a deliberately slow pace. The wet, tight glide of her pussy was an evil torture on a dick that had needed to fuck the hell out of her since I saw her outside the gallery.

I floated between heaven and hell.

"Eli?"

"What?"

I inhaled deep, trying not to dig my fingers into the soft round flesh of her ass, wanting desperately to give it to her the way I desired.

"Do you know how much I crave your cock?" she purred into my ear.

She was a witch possessed by Aphrodite or Peitho. Both goddesses were wicked seductresses.

I threw my head back. "Stop talking and fuck me."

"I am." She licked up the side of my neck and rubbed her cheek along mine while continuing that incessantly slow pace. "Answer the question."

"I know. We barely keep our hands off each other."

"Does this mean you crave my pussy too?" She arched, rolled her hips, and positioned her breasts right in front of my eyes.

Her breasts were so full, and her nipples were hard and ready for my bite.

"I know what you're doing. That's cheating."

"I'm fucking you. Isn't that what you wanted?" Avra smirked, but a deep flush bloomed over her skin.

That was it. Avra had hit the point where her body required a push to send her over. I knew the meaning of every sigh, every change in breath, even the slightest change in her coloring when it came to sex.

"You won't come at this pace, Avra."

"We're in a challenge. I will win."

Her unsteady breath tugged at this part of me that demanded I satisfy her. The hairs on the back of my neck prickled.

"I'm ordering you to make yourself come."

"I don't take orders very well." She closed her eyes, her orgasm teetering but still out of reach.

I smacked her ass, causing her to jerk and quiver around me.

"That's cheating," she shouted.

I gritted my teeth, losing the battle not to rail until she begged for mercy.

"Make yourself come, or I will do it for you."

She stopped her movement with a frown. "Why is it so important? This is just a game."

Why couldn't she understand its logic? It was simple.

"You're my fucking wife. It's my job to see to your pleasure." I gripped her forearms. "What idiot doesn't care for the most important thing in their life?"

She gaped at me. "Why do you have to say shit like this? I was already in love with you."

It was my turn to stare open-mouthed at her. She couldn't mean it. We fought, we laughed, we fucked.

Our marriage was a business, arranged, nothing more.

Who was I kidding?

I shifted, turning us so she sat on the seat. "Do you mean it?"

"Mean what?" She looked around. "You moved. I win."

I gripped her jaw and leaned in. "That you love me."

"Why is this a surprise?" She swallowed. "I thought you knew the night we made our deal."

She wrapped her arms around me, drawing me to her. She brushed her lips across mine, soft and gentle. But there was something to it that felt as if she'd punched me in the gut. However, I wanted more of it.

She pulled back, and her gaze locked with mine.

After a few seconds, she said, "I never planned to marry. I accepted that a husband and children weren't possible, at least for me. I lived in hiding, and any dreams I had vanished after the coup. Then, this plan came into existence, and I decided an arranged marriage was better than nothing. I wasn't prepared for you. I wasn't prepared for this."

A tear slid down her cheek. And this confirmed it. I was utterly lost to this woman.

How the fuck had that happened?

I loved my wife.

"Neither was I." I cupped her face. "I meant what I said."

"You've said a lot of things."

"I'm possessive, Avra—to a dangerous level. You're mine. That means something to me. I will protect you."

Her lips turned up at the corners. "Well then, possessive man. Are you planning to fuck me or put that delicious hard cock to waste?"

"That mouth of yours will result in some severe consequences." I fisted myself at the base and aligned myself with her.

"You like my mouth." She wrapped her legs around my waist and pushed her wet pussy onto me, taking me all the way to the hilt and making me hiss. "Especially when I deep-throat you and swallow."

"Shut up and let me fuck you." I pulled out and surged back in, hard and rough, just as she liked it.

She moaned and rolled her hips. She pulled me closer, her arms looping under mine and holding tight.

"Fuck me hard, Eli. Don't hold back. I want you to release the beast inside you. Please. Let me feel you everywhere."

"Don't complain tomorrow," I growled, lifting her by the waist and keeping my cock buried deep in her. I carried her into the bedroom, not giving a shit about the water. As soon as we reached the bed, I set her on the end and reached for the cords hidden along the edges. I tied her arms and splayed her open for me. Her pussy glistened, and my cock was covered with her arousal.

I set a hard, unrelenting pace, loving the sight of my dick pistoning in and out of her.

My fingers clutched her hips and jerked her into the

thrust of my hips, giving her no control. This wasn't anywhere near romantic or gentle, but vicious, dark, unforgiving, and perfect. Her clit teased me, so swollen, so exposed, calling me to taste, to tease.

She was my fucking addiction.

Her pussy flexed, and the muscles all but sucked me with each pass, testing my stamina and will. It was too much, and I couldn't hold off much longer.

I jerked out of her.

"No." She cried out and then gasped, and my lips closed over her beautiful, exposed, swollen pearl.

I laved her pussy, giving her no chance to think of anything beyond the sensation coursing throughout her body. She tossed her head from side to side, and her bound hands clenched into fists against her inner thighs.

The second she released little mewled whimpers, I thrust three fingers inside her, and she detonated, her back bowing and neck arching. There never was such a beautiful sight.

I crawled over her and plunged deep, lucky enough to catch the remainder of her orgasm.

She gazed up at me through a haze of pleasure, and barely above a whisper, she said, "I do love you, even if I didn't want to."

Those words snapped what little of my restraint I had left. I fucked her like a madman, wanting nothing more than to imprint my cock in her beautiful cunt. At the same time, her arousal rose again, and she lifted her hips, trying to meet my intense thrusts. My balls drew up. It was over for me. She felt just too damn good.

Sliding my fingers to her clit, I circled her, teased, and right before I came, I pinched, pushing her over. The contractions of her cunt shot me into my release, and it was the best thing I'd ever felt.

My wife. The woman I loved. She was giving herself to me.

I would destroy anyone who dared to hurt her.

TWENTY-ONE

vra

"Avra, are you home?" Laya asked me the second I answered my mobile.

"Yes. You sound upset. What's wrong?"

"Are you alone?"

"Why? Did something happen to you?"

"It's important. I have to talk to you. Vik should be there soon."

I frowned. "Vik's coming over? What's going on, Laya? You're scaring me."

"I can't talk about it like this. Just tell me if Eli is there?"

"No, he's at meetings all day with his men."

She heaved an audible, exasperated sigh. "What about his

people? Are any of them around? I don't want anyone there who can report back to him."

A chill slid down my spine.

"You're seriously scaring me. Why don't you want any of the Xenoses around?"

"Because it is Vitalis business," she shouted. "Is that clear enough?"

Something big had to be wrong for her to act this way.

"Does it have to do with Eli?" I asked, knowing her answer already.

A lump formed in the pit of my stomach, and all the contentment and joy I'd felt over the last week or so evaporated. We'd come so far. Even this morning, he mentioned trying for a child as soon as this mess with his father was settled.

What could have happened?

Vik walked through the door with a folder held under his arm and gestured with his chin. "Layana?"

"Yes." I nodded.

"She called me too."

I returned to Laya. "Let me guess, you told him everything."

"Of course. His information corroborates with mine. I'm nearly there." She hung up, leaving me with an empty line.

Corroborates? What the fuck was that supposed to mean?

Vik took the phone from me, encased it in a box, and then pulled out a small device, which I recognized as an electronics barrier and scrambler meant to prevent any listening or monitoring equipment from working.

Shit, shit, shit. This was bad.

"We need to go to your office right now."

Without another word, I led him down the hall. The second we entered, Vik threw the folder on top of my desk and went to work, searching everywhere.

"Wait to open that." His gaze landed on me, and then he ordered, "Look for a camera like I taught you."

I scoured the area around me. Eli wouldn't invade my privacy. I trusted him.

Why would he spy on me?

My heart hammered as I waited for Vic to finish his inspection.

"Does this concern Caras, Bella, and Korba?" I asked.

"Yes and no."

"What kind of answer is that?"

He stared at me with his calm, unwavering eyes. "The kind telling you to sit your ass in the chair and wait. And don't open that folder."

Releasing a deep, centering breath, I closed my eyes briefly before holding his gaze.

He was my second father. I would not lose my shit on him. However, he needed a reminder of a few things.

"I am the Vitalis, yes or no?"

He nodded. "Yes."

"Then you answer to me, yes or no?"

"Yes." His lips tightened, not liking where these questions were going.

"Then answer my fucking question. What did Laya say to you?"

"She said to get to your place and ensure you are alone. If not, find a way to get you to leave."

"Why?"

"Because she is going to tell you a story about the trust, Ozias Xenos, Eli, and your death. Once she is done, I will show you something, and you will decide."

"What does that mean?" I asked, taking my seat.

A pounding erupted in my head, almost as if it had a pulse of its own. Anger bubbled up inside me, and my skin heated.

Eli loved me. The last thing he would do was conspire with his father.

I wouldn't make rash assumptions and wait for Laya to give the details. My heart refused to listen and screamed as if it had just shattered into pieces.

I couldn't allow my emotions to overwhelm me. So, I pushed everything back, donned a calm mask, and waited for Vik's reply.

"Exactly as I stated. Laya arrives, she gives the information, I add mine, you ask your questions, and then you decide the next course of action."

A lump formed in the pit of my stomach. "If what I'm sensing is accurate, I won't have any choice in my next steps."

"Are you saying you would walk away from a happy marriage?"

I leaned forward. "I'm saying I will kill him for betraying me."

I would cry and mourn him, but it would happen.

"You are definitely Juno's daughter."

"Is that an insult or a compliment?"

He smirked. "Both."

A car pulled up to the house, and a minute later, Laya rushed through my office door, closed it, and pressed her back to it as she gasped for air.

Once she caught her breath, she asked, "Are you sure Elias isn't here?"

I shook my head. "He's off to a meeting."

She glanced at Vik. "Are any of Elias's men around?"

I answered for him. "They've gone with him. Only our people are guarding the home now."

She nodded and moved to the seat near Vik, turning to him. "Can I assume you did the scanning, and it's clean in here?"

Vik gestured to me, and Laya scowled.

"It's clean. I want the story. Don't stop unless I ask you a question."

"Oh shit." Laya's eyes widened. "You've gone into that facts-only mode."

"Start talking, Layana."

She sighed, her face sad, and said, "Ozias Xenos accepted the marriage offer without question because he knew about the trust in Switzerland and the fact all Vitalis lands belong to us."

Vik shook his head.

I narrowed my gaze. "You suspected this and didn't say anything?"

"I didn't have proof until recently." He glanced at the folder. "I've kept my eyes on Xenos from the beginning. When I finally had something to show, Laya brought her information."

I turned my attention back to Laya. "Keep going."

"Ozias has known about it for years," Laya continued, "but he couldn't touch it because of the Vitalis clause. He knows the family heads in Boston oversee the trust and would have stopped him if he dared to touch it."

"Of course," I muttered. "The greedy bastard wasn't satisfied. Too bad for him, Papa knew how to manage his estate and finances. Keep going. I know it gets worse."

"Do you remember how you described him after that first dinner? Like you belonged to him, not Eli. How he believed he was some king?" I nodded, and she added. "You're the key to making him one. His plan was for you to marry Eli and become pregnant. Then he would eliminate us."

I finished her story. "And after I deliver my child, he plans to find some way to kill me, leaving him with a grandchild who owns all the Vitalis lands and the trust, free and clear."

"Exactly. Killing the three assholes in the wine bar also made it easier for Ozias to seize their land since it belongs to a Vitalis."

"How did you discover this information?"

"You don't believe me." She narrowed her eyes. "Why would I lie about something like this?"

"For fuck's sake, Laya. You're not a liar. I'd like to know

how you discovered this information. Did you verify that the source is credible?"

"Are you kidding me right now? Anyone who knows about the trust and the land threatens us. I'm not stupid enough to believe anything unless I hear it with my own ears."

That's when Vik jumped in, not giving two shits about my order. "I'm curious about this too. Where the fuck did you go, and where was your detail?"

Laya ignored Vik, scooted to the chair's edge, and faced me. "I went out with some locals who don't know who I am. I pretended to be just some ordinary girl. To blend in, I dressed like a college kid out on the town."

"Seriously, Laya. You complained about disguising yourself in Prague, and now you do it to go barhopping?"

"I hated feeling like I had to hide in Prague. There is a big difference." She scoffed. "Do you want the details or not?"

This was not the time for a lecture. I would save that for another day.

"All right."

She nodded. "I stumbled upon some of Ozias's men. I recognized them from the wedding. They were out drinking and partying, and they had no idea who I was."

"And they just blurted out all of that information?" I asked.

"No. Once I figured out who the men were, I stuck around, flirted, and got them talking. They're men. Give them some attention, make them feel big and strong, keep them drinking, and give them the impression one of them will hit it with you." Laya shrugged. "The usual. Once they were falling all over themselves to impress me, I asked about their jobs and fawned over them. They seemed new and young. Probably too inexperienced to know when to shut up. I convinced them that I was so curious about all the excitement they had in their world, working for Ozias."

"Did they say Eli was part of this?"

"Most said they weren't sure since father and son hate each other, but a couple of them insisted it was an act." Laya reached over my desk and covered my hand that I'd placed on top of hers. "I didn't want to believe them, even if I heard it. So, I called Vik early this morning."

Vik spoke. "Open the folder, Avra. Take a look inside. As you know, I've had some of our people watching him from the start. He isn't as opposed to his father's antics as he would have you believe."

Sliding my palm from Laya's, I followed Vik's instructions and found pictures of Eli meeting with men who were Ozias's enforcers. His second was with him. The interactions were friendly as if the public dislike was all an act. There were multiple meetings at various locations.

"As you see, they met several times. He's a good actor," Vik added.

I focused on the date in the corner of a picture. It was the day of the gallery incident when he found me after Francesca's attack. That was the meeting he'd come from.

"Why didn't you show me these before today?" I met Vik's gaze.

"Because it isn't enough proof he was doing anything wrong."

My gut told me he was holding back something. "What aren't you telling me?"

He pulled out his phone. "This isn't a clear video considering the angle of the recording, but you can hear the conversation. It's from the last meeting."

Voice 1: Make sure you have everyone in position.

Voice 2: Does she suspect you're planning this?

Eli: No, and I will do everything to make sure it stays that way.

Voice 2: You're dead if she finds out.

Eli chuckles: I know. I'm late. Keep to the plan.

Voice 1: Don't forget. Ozias wants her sisters first, then your wife.

Eli: Make sure you're ready. I know my role.

The recording stopped, and we sat in silence.

He'd played me. A heavy weight settled on my shoulders, and there was nothing else to do but move forward.

"I'm sorry, Avra." Vik's voice conveyed nothing but disappointment. "I've never seen you so happy. The last thing I would do is take it from you, especially not like this."

"You didn't do this. Neither of you did. You saved us." I stared, seeing nothing but a haze before me. Then, my mind cleared. I wanted to hear the whole conversation. What else had he said about me?

"Is there more to the recording?"

"That's all the soldiers sent me."

I gritted my teeth. "Send it to my phone."

"You already have it."

I nodded and stared down at the photos again.

I'd believed him, trusted him, opened my heart, and fell in love with him.

How could he stoop so far and low to make a fool out of me?

Yes, fucking was part of marriage but tricking me into imagining this could be real between us. Not an arranged marriage like a business transaction, but one with emotions and connection.

Laya's information, the pictures, and the recording lined up too perfectly to be coincidences.

No matter how much I wished for it, I couldn't pretend away the truth.

"Avra," Vik said in a tone I hadn't heard since that night so long ago.

The night I lost my parents and the only home I'd ever known.

"Go to your room and take a few moments. Even your Papa allowed himself to grieve betrayal."

Not saying anything, I took the folder and moved down the hallway leading into my bedroom, going straight to the bathroom vanity.

I gazed at my reflection.

I should have known.

I should have fucking known something like this would happen.

Does he laugh at me behind my back? Is he smug and

amused that I fell for his father's plan? Of course, he is—I heard it during that conversation.

My soul cried, parts of it refusing to believe the reality of this situation. I wanted to cling to the warm moments of security and love Eli had started to show me as a possibility for our future.

I wanted to go back. If only I could reverse time, not just to the barriers we broke in the tub, but further, before I shared anything with Eli except my body.

I could only blame myself for falling for it. I had allowed myself to believe Eli and I could have what Mama and Papa shared. Those were stupid childhood fantasies, nothing more.

You're a fucking fool, Avra.

The second I heard his car arrive, then the hum of the garage door, I straightened my back. Pulling a tissue from the box before me, I wiped my tears away.

I couldn't break. I refused to break in front of him.

Rage filled me, battering my bleeding, shattered heart. I may have fallen for it, but Eli had manipulated me, used me, and made me believe we'd grow old together.

I clenched my jaw, fisted the folder in my fingers, and stalked through my room and into the hallway, livid with myself that I'd lost sight of what mattered—keeping my enemies close —and let Elias distract me from what Ozias wanted.

Control.

He'd never stop until he had my entire family six feet under.

"Avra, don't do it like this," I heard Vik say from behind me. "You need a clear mind."

Then Laya spoke. "Call the men. This scene is going to be bad."

Bad wasn't the word I'd use.

"I want all of you to stay out of sight," I commanded. "Do you hear me?"

"We hear you, but we're staying within listening range. Our men will be with us," Vik responded.

I let out a deep breath. That was exactly what I expected.

I waited in the front entryway. All the staff seemed to have vanished. Given the mood shift in the house, it was the safest course for them.

My whole body shook, fury igniting every nerve in me. Cold, unemotional logic was my approach with him. Then I would walk away.

As soon as I saw him step inside, my plan to remain calm disappeared. The wrath bubbling up in my veins erupted, and I charged at him.

I kept my arms at my sides, not trusting myself to avoid clocking him. I wanted to hurt him, make him feel a mere ounce of the pain I felt because of his actions.

"How could you lie to me all along?" I screamed. "Why did you make me believe?"

"Avra?" He held his hands up, stepping back with utter confusion on his face. "What's going on?"

I was too devastated to think straight. If I were any weaker, I'd crumple and drop, sobbing into the carpet as I pounded my hand to the surface.

Instead, I shoved the agony and tears back and faced him directly. "You lied to me over and over. How could you?"

"How could I what?" He looked around me as if expecting others, and then returned to me. "What did I do?"

"How could you make me love you, knowing that you would destroy my world and take everything from me?"

"What?" His eyes widened, and a crease formed between his brows.

He shook his head as if needing a moment to let my question sink in.

When he finally spoke, his words came out as if he was in disbelief. "I did what?"

"How could you marry me and make me feel—" I stopped myself, not wanting to repeat how I felt and endure the pain of it, so I asked, "How could you align with me only to take everything away?"

"I have no fucking idea about anything you are saying."

"You do!" I shoved the folder against his chest, wishing he could have the decency to be honest now. "Explain this. Tell me you weren't laughing and making plans with Ozias's people while pretending with me."

He stared at the pictures, shaking his head. "I can explain these. There is a reason for these."

"What explanation can you give me that I will remotely believe?"

"They're my men."

I threw my hands in the air. "Of course, they are your men. Xenos men. They belong to you and your father."

As if trying to calm an excited beast, he moved slowly

into the house, taking measured steps. "No, they are mine. Not Ozias's. They are my eyes and ears around him. I swear to you. I have nothing to do with whatever you heard."

The sincerity of his words slapped me in a way that was worse than any physical hurt I'd ever experienced.

"I saw the recording of your last meeting. You were laughing about me killing you if I found out."

"Recording? Whatever you saw was wrong. They updated me on Ozias, and I gave them orders for my other men."

"You want me to believe you meet with them nearly every week only for updates on Ozias?"

Eli cocked his head to the side. "What other reasons were you given? And how do you know I'm meeting with them that often? Are you having me followed?"

"Does it truly matter? Given what I've learned, trusting you seems like the worst choice I could make."

"Avra. If something is planned or going on, I have nothing to do with it." He stepped closer, but when I glared at him, he stilled. "I haven't betrayed you in any way."

"I can't trust you. I heard what you said, and others did too."

"Whatever that was, it wasn't the truth. Every plan I've made is to protect you."

"I don't believe you."

He sighed and lowered his head. "I swear on my mother's place in heaven. I would never do anything to hurt you."

Twenty-Two

E lias

Avra gasped. "You can't make vows with your mother's soul."

"Then how can I get you to believe me?" I asked her.

Seeing her look at me as her enemy again felt as if something had pierced my soul.

Having her bombard me with her anger and fury was one thing. Still, the energy of utter hurt, pain, and betrayal around her frightened me.

Losing her wasn't an option.

Whoever took those pictures, made that recording, and fed those thoughts to her about me would face a long, agonizing death. They knew nothing of the lengths I'd go for her.

My people had risked their lives to uncover all of Ozias's plans. They had formed an extra shield between him and Avra.

Everything inside me churned, and I couldn't control any of it. I hated this feeling and never wanted to experience it again.

We'd made a deal, yes. However, it was a ruse to cover what we actually wanted—a future together, one where we chose each other.

I had to make it right.

"I don't understand any of this. I want to trust you." Her voice broke as she swallowed down her tears.

Seeing her so heartbroken and wounded wrecked a part of me I never knew existed until her.

Each time she looked away, as though the mere sight of me was too much to stomach, I felt as if I'd fallen into the most bottomless pit of hell.

But I couldn't fight her on this. I couldn't fix something I had no hand in.

Ozias.

It was the only explanation. He took my mother from me, and now he wanted Avra.

Over my dead body.

"Can you tell me what the recording said?" I reached out to take her hands, but she crossed her arms, refusing my touch.

I replayed her heated words, trying to understand what could have turned her against me.

Then I remembered her asking, *"How could you make me love you knowing that you would destroy my world and take everything from me?"*

Why would I do any of those things?

That was bullshit.

Lies and nonsense.

I ran a frustrated hand through my hair. "I want a future *with* you. I don't want to ruin or steal anything. I'll never rob you of anything."

Her green eyes shined bright with so much doubt.

"I'm committed to our marriage." I held up the hand with the ring she slid on my finger at our wedding.

"So long as your father deems it necessary."

Fuck. Ozias.

I fisted my hand and lowered it. I would never forgive Ozias for destroying everything I built with Avra. "I won't be a part of anything my father is trying to accomplish."

She snorted and looked away for a second. "Until you get your child. Then you'll get rid of me."

How could she believe that bullshit?

I lunged forward, taking her hand. She stiffened and then tried to jerk out of my hold, but I held firmly and tugged until she was near me.

"Let me go," she hissed.

"Not until you hear me." I glared down at her. "And by hearing me, I mean listening to my words."

She blew out a frustrated breath and muttered, "Just say it."

"That thought"—I lowered my face to hers, staring straight into her eyes— "never entered my mind."

She parted her lips, gazing at me so openly as if she wanted to accept my words.

But the doubt remained, burning bright.

These wounds she believed I had caused festered so deep. All I could do was give all I had to heal them.

This woman fucking owned me and couldn't see it.

"I want a future with you. Children and then grandchildren. Generations to follow us as we grow old together."

Her lips trembled, and a whirlwind of dark emotions played over her face. She lowered her chin, dropping her gaze to my chest.

I couldn't let her hide from this. We had to fix it.

"Our future is together." I cupped her face, lifting it back up. "I'll accept never having a child if it means having you always with me."

Her eyes widened in complete disbelief. "You would give up having children to pass down your name, your legacy?"

Again, she tried to glance away as though it was too hard to hear me, but I refused to let her budge.

"Each time I saw you in danger, I felt as though I was losing my mind. First, with the idiot on the street, then during the standoff with you and Pello, and then when you publicly handled Francesca. Why can't you see that the idea of not having you with me is too unbearable to think about? Let me hear this recording that has condemned me."

"All right, you want to hear it. Listen and then explain it back to me." She grabbed her phone and played the recording.

My heart sank. To anyone who heard it, it sounded like I was plotting against Avra and her family. Each word, stripped of the true meaning and context of my orders, left me vulnerable to all of Avra's accusations.

"Now tell me it's a lie." The pain in her green eyes pierced deeper than the earlier icy stare.

All I could do was offer her the truth.

"I was instructing my men in Ozias's camp to prepare for a coup. My intelligence made me suspicious that Ozias was planning something against your sisters, and I wanted to act first. I don't expect you to believe me, but I would give up everything I have, everything I am, to protect you and yours."

"Eli, don't say things like that. This hurts so much as it is." She shook her head, wrenching free.

I wouldn't give up, and I followed her as she escaped to the living room. I blocked her before she could close the door and lock me out.

She walked away from me, went to the farthest sofa near the window, and sat, covering her face with her palms.

I followed her, kneeling on the carpet before her, and tugged her hands down.

I waited until she lifted her gaze to mine. The emotions of moments earlier seemed null in her irises. An unreachable, detached void stared at me.

No. No. No.

She had to hear me. I had to get through to her.

"There's been enough bloodshed in your family. All because of *mine*. But I would never add to it. I would never want to involve myself in something designed to hurt or bring you down."

"We are born enemies," she stated without any inflection.

"Our family ties made us that way. Our marriage changed —" I broke off, thinking of the right words. "We are something else."

A tinge of sadness tunneled through me as the realization hit me. If Avra walked away, would I survive this?

"I want to burn down the world for you, with you, and nothing will make me change my mind. Not even my father."

She shook her head, tracing her fingertip on mine, the barest touch of something like affection. Her shoulders remained stiff, showing me how much this disconnect between us pulled on her physically.

"I'm..." She took a deep breath. "I'm confused by the recording. Your words felt so cold and calculating. The way you laughed while discussing me."

"My men often joke that if I pushed you too far, you wouldn't hesitate to slice my throat. They find every chance to mention it. They became your biggest fans after the day you told me to make it hurt following that incident with the little girl and that idiot who ran away."

She shook her head. "I don't know what to think."

Please tell me what you feel. I refused to think it had all been a lie. It couldn't evaporate in an instant. What we shared, the barriers we'd broken down, and the vulnerability we allowed only with each other weren't things done frivo- lously. They meant something to us.

She loved me. She said she loved me.

"Don't think," I argued as gently as I could. "*Know* that I'm telling you the truth. Know that I love you."

"You love me?" she asked with shock in her tone as she stared at me, her head cocked slightly and a crease forming between her brows.

Why was she surprised by this?

I couldn't believe she was unprepared to hear those words, especially after the other night in the bathtub.

I squeezed her hand. "I mean it. I love you, Avra. The last thing I want to do is ruin what we have and what we are building. I will never want to hurt you."

When she closed her eyes and sighed, it told me every- thing I needed to know. She still didn't believe me.

I poured my heart and soul out to her and kneeled before her, and it wasn't enough.

The knowledge that she couldn't trust my words shredded my soul.

"I will prove it." I stood.

She remained on the couch. "Eli, what are you doing?"

The immediate worry in her voice showed the first traces of emotion since she sat.

"Like I said. I'll prove I'm telling you the truth. I'm going to speak to my father right now."

"This doesn't make sense."

I looked at her. "I'll tell you what makes no sense. I'm the villain in a story I didn't even know I belonged in, and since Ozias is at the root of this, I'll find out from the source."

I should have dug deep into Ozias's business. I was well aware he planned something, but putting my name into anything went too fucking far.

"You truly don't know?"

I clenched my jaw as I reached the living room door. "It is all I've tried to get you to believe since I walked through the fucking door."

"Eli." She stepped in my direction, and I raised my hand, telling her to stop.

"No, I never want any doubt between us. I swear it to you now. On my life, on my mother's place in heaven, I will never help him with his pursuits. I would never do anything to hurt you."

I turned, stalking through the house and heading to the garage. Once in the car, I tore down the road.

I would reach that son of a bitch as fast as possible.

Visions of killing him with my bare hands filled my mind, choking him, watching his eyes bulge and the veins on his face and in his eyes burst.

My fingers flexed with every scenario of death I played out, each one more violent than the last.

As I approached the estate, I sent a few voice messages to my top lieutenants telling them to gather every scrap of information circulating about Ozias. I wanted rumors, gossip, any tiny mention of that fucker's name.

I ran the family, and they obeyed me. Ozias had his little team, but everyone around him knew the truth.

Years of work, of proving myself, of dealing with the same shit as my soldiers garnered loyalty my father could never think of receiving. In a war between us, he'd come out the loser.

His ego kept him from accepting truths. Now, he'd face facts.

He was my genetic donor only, never a parent, and not a father in any form or fashion. I was his son. But he wasn't my boss. He'd ceased earning my respect when I was a child. He'd been the recipient of my loathing since the day he struck my mother. And since the day he killed Eudora Vitalis, he'd been on my shit list, one of the people I'd love to see suffer and beg for mercy.

I pressed my foot on the pedal harder, despising every mile that made up the distance between me and Ozias. I wanted to be at his stupid house now. I wanted to get this over with and return to Avra.

I was coming for answers.

And no matter the risk, the costs be damned, I would stop whatever bullshit schemes he wanted to put into play.

My wife came first.

Always.

It was time to show her how much I meant that.

TWENTY-THREE

Once Elias left the house, Vik and Laya slowly exited my office. It was apparent that they heard everything said between Eli and me—his declaration of love, his claim that he could never hurt me, and that vow.

My throat burned thinking of it.

So many thoughts and so many emotions tumbled around in my mind. The flowers set on the low table before me were a blurry haze.

He'd looked so broken when he left.

I'd done that to him. He wasn't the type to beg, and he'd knelt before me, pleading for me to listen to him.

He expected me to believe him innocent in this. And

everything inside me wanted to, oh, how it tried to do just that.

"Avra." Vik cleared his throat.

This was just too much.

Trust him or don't?

Believe him or stand firm?

"Avra," Vik called my name again, but this time with a harsher tone, snapping me out of the pit I found myself drowning within.

I looked at Vik. Instead of feeling discomfort for over-hearing Eli and me exchange emotional words, I felt his compassion and understanding.

"Don't make rash decisions while in this state." He held my gaze and then said, "I will check in with the team and alert them to this news. I'm going to get the full recording."

With that, he turned and walked away. He would find the truth, whatever it was.

This man, who raised me, someone who wasn't one for hugs or loving words, had given me more emotions in the last hour than I'd received from him in years. Maybe he'd walled himself off to protect himself as I had done.

I nodded, even though he couldn't see me, and then turned my attention to Laya as she entered my line of sight. As Eli had crouched in front of me, she perched on the edge of the low table.

I sighed so heavily that it took all my strength not to sob. It was the one thing I hadn't allowed myself to do since losing Mama and Papa. A tear here or there was one thing, but breaking down, crying my eyes out, and allowing the pain locked inside me to rush out wasn't something I allowed.

As the eldest, I stayed strong, protected my sisters, and gave them hope for a better future.

Except, I couldn't muster a tiny grain of strength to do any of it.

If only the numbness I'd used to allow to overtake my emotions would work now.

Fuck, I've really lost sight of the plan.

All because of Elias Xenos. Because of how he made me feel and believe we could have something like real love.

Laya took my hands in hers. "That wasn't how I expected things to go."

"Queen of understatements as always, Layana."

"What do you think?" she asked me.

I lifted a brow as if she had asked me to define the meaning of life. "I have a lot of thoughts. Why don't you ask a more specific question?"

"Do you think Elias knows about any of it?" She furrowed her brow, and then her features softened as though it pained her to ask this. "Do you think he's in on his father's plans to deceive you?"

I firmed my lips in a tight press. "I don't know. From the start, we both went in knowing our marriage was nothing more than a means to an end. A game of deception wrapped up in a business transaction."

She nodded. "An act."

"Yes."

"You said *was*. Not *is*."

"Things changed, Laya. Now, I don't know what to think." The back of my throat burned. "It's hard to accept all of it was a lie. That recording. None of it makes sense."

I thought back to all of my times with him. Each one painted a poignant moment of intimacy. It wasn't about the intense and addictive sex but the mundane things. Every time we'd shared a meal and talked about business, theories, and life in general. Just being with him had become so much more than a charade. Living with and waking up beside him every morning represented a deep commitment I never wanted to lose.

If this truly was one-sided, then I wasn't sure how I'd overcome the heartache.

"Well..." Laya sucked in a long breath as if shoring up her courage to continue speaking.

Or maybe she searched for the best words to offer me. She was the one I leaned on for tough sisterly talks. Cali was the strategic one, and having her in the mix for business and planning came in handy. However, she was too soft and prone to emotions in such situations.

Vik was cold and analytical, and knowing how uncomfortable tears made him, I wouldn't turn to him for this situation unless we waged war. Laya was more like me, balancing both, keeping her heart safe behind walls and staying tough on the outside.

"Well, what?"

She smiled sadly. "Well, maybe there's more to what Eli said than what you're telling yourself to believe. What if it all was a setup?"

"That's where my thoughts keep going, but everything lines up. I don't know *what* to believe. Or who."

She frowned, a crease forming between her brows.

"I know you aren't lying. So get that murderous glare off your face." I huffed.

"Then stop talking and hear me out." She gestured at herself. "I'll be the devil's advocate for a moment here."

I smirked. "Go right ahead."

"And I'll be honest. I didn't like Elias at first."

"Because he is the son of Mama's murderer?"

"That." She rested her elbows on her knees for a beat. "He was just so...harsh at first. I swore the man couldn't smile, not even fake it."

Because he's not a fake man, he is—was—real. What you saw was what you got with Elias. Or so I'd been duped into believing.

"He had this inner darkness, this lethal vibe, and yeah, it did make me uneasy to think of you being stuck with him, within reach if he were to be abusive like so many husbands can be."

I shook my head. "He's a hard man, but not toward me."

Any and all bruises or marks he left on my body were the result of unhinged, carnal lust and pure, uninhibited desire.

I'd keep that information to myself, or it would derail the conversation.

"After you returned from your honeymoon, I saw that. Elias made you happy, physically, at least. Do you remember that lunch? You couldn't stop blushing. *No* man has ever made you blush or smile so carefree like that, no one until him. And you can't fake that."

I nodded, my cheeks heating, thinking about how I must have looked that day from her perspective.

"I figured he was hung and knew how to use it. Yay for Avra." She gave me a mocking fist pump.

I glared at her. "Really?"

"Shh. I'm still talking." She put a finger to her lips. "What proved that he cared about those *you* cared about was when he sent his men to back up ours, ensuring we were protected here. Then he arranged the whole thing for you with the trio. Those were his father's friends. He went *against* his father's allies. That's pretty cut and dried. If he were working with Ozias, I can't see him serving up his friends for you to slaughter."

She was right. That didn't add up in any other way.

"Not only that. I've studied the way he watches you. You've had my back for fifteen years, Avra. Mine and Cali's. Hell, even Vik's. You are a protector."

I stared at her, wishing I could take faith in whatever observations she would share with me.

"Elias does for you what you do for us—always keeping an eye on you, watching you. Your comfort is his priority. He genuinely cares if you're happy."

"But his father...and the video."

"Let me address each one separately. His father is an evil asshole. Him. Not Elias. Ozias is a bastard we need to put down. But Elias is not his father."

I liked her comparison, separating the two. The more she

elaborated on her opinions, the more swayed I was to believe her.

"And the recording," she continued. "I'm suspicious why we only have that small clip, not the whole conversation. Doesn't it make you wonder why the soldier didn't want us to see and hear the whole thing?"

"Vik will have the answer to that question soon enough," I said, looking down at the rings on my left hand. "And for Eli, I will know the truth based on how he handles this situation with Ozias. He'll prove you wrong if he follows his father's orders."

"And if he doesn't?" she pressed. "If he stops or tries to prevent his father from seeing his plan through?"

"Then I'll reconsider and have faith that he does love me."

Layana smiled a bit wider, pleased. She patted my knee. "I respect that. Given the circumstances and how hard we've worked and planned to get to this point, I would decide the same."

"Thank you." Her support helped.

"I mean, *I've* never been in love. It looks like I won't have a chance to discover it, but I can imagine that maybe love overrules hate in some regards."

I hope so. I badly wanted to think that Elias's love would triumph over anything his father wanted him to do or go along with.

Deep down, I wanted so strongly to trust my husband. I yearned to believe him after all we'd managed to build. He'd broken down and smashed apart so many barriers to my heart, and now all of this. It was cruel. It was unfair. And I hated that I wanted to stomp and rage that both circumstances shouldn't interfere with my future.

Because that alternative was too bitter and sour of a reality to accept, now that I'd let Elias in and given him carefully dosed-out permission to creep into my heart and mind, it would be far more painful to endure the aftermath of not having him so close.

"How mad will Cali be at us for leaving her out of this discussion? I'm sure she will have some choice words."

I rolled my eyes. "If by choice, you mean the colorful string of acronyms I can't decipher. I'm sure she will."

"Actually..." She frowned, glancing at her phone. "I haven't heard from her at all today."

That wasn't like her. She kept us in the loop on everything.

"She wasn't at the house?" I checked.

She shrugged. "Well, I wasn't either. Vik and I were out talking, and then I went out last night, pretending to be a college girl, and ended up with too many secrets to keep to myself. I slept in after the drinking"—at my glare, she sighed—"not that much drinking. Still, I thought waiting until today to tell you would make more sense. I didn't want to barge into the 'just married and we like to fuck in the kitchen' house that late to talk."

"Are you kidding me?"

She shrugged. "The staff knows it all, Avra."

"The house was empty," I surmised.

"Keep believing that..." Laya looked at her phone again, scrolling through her texts. "She didn't message. That's not like her at all."

I grabbed my phone to see when I last spoke with her. Texts were our go-to, not calls, but still—

I snapped into sister mode, my attention squarely back to a protector duty. Cali didn't often wander and strike off on her own. Someone would always tail her. Security was a given. Even if she wanted to be alone, she was more of a homebody, preferring books and sketching in her notebooks than taking off and getting out.

"I forgot. We were going to meet up, but she changed plans and said something about an information session on upcoming classes at the university library."

Laya smiled. "Yeah. And I'm pretty sure she said something to me yesterday morning about books on loan."

We shared a knowing look. Cali at a library? She needed a tracker in a building full of books.

Laya got up, tilting her head toward the kitchen. "How about we make something to eat before you start overthinking everything? There is nothing you can do without more information."

I got to my feet, appreciating her offer to keep me company.

"Unless I'm overstaying..."

I grabbed her hand and led her to the kitchen. "Not at all. I must stay preoccupied and not dwell on whether I'll still want to keep my husband."

I do.

My motives had to stay contingent on what he decided with his father first.

Twenty-Four

E lias

I arrived at my father's house, alarmed and annoyed at the abundance of vehicles parked out front. At first, I worried he was calling a meeting for strategic reasons. And then, I reminded myself how out of character that would have been.

Ozias wasn't current on the protocols for organizing a formal gathering of the lieutenants. Things ran completely differently since I'd taken over, and someone would have informed me the moment the old directives passed through the ranks.

No matter, something was going on. A party, perhaps. Whatever it was, I planned to crash this wonderful event, and no one would fucking stop me. I planned to get answers. If an audience awaited, so be it.

They'd get a fucking show.

I couldn't lose Avra. And I would protect her and her sisters.

Before I got through the front foyer, I was beckoned to the side by one of Ozias's lieutenants, Stephanos. Technically, he was one of my men woven into my father's team. For the last week, he'd left messages to meet, but nothing was secure. Now, I regretted not making a better effort to collect his information, especially considering a convenient recording passing into Avra's hands.

"Sir." He glanced toward the back patio before tipping his head to the side.

From the distant sounds of music and laughter over conversations, I figured that was where my father was. I followed Stephanos, though, curious what he could have learned here at the bastard's home.

I nodded at him, giving him silent permission to speak. "Some fresh recruits came to me saying they heard a few higher-level recruits talking about plans that didn't sit well with them."

"Go on."

"They were flirting with some girl and then bragged about how they were part of a plan to take your child and kill your wife and her sisters."

I sucked in a sharp breath.

"That's what she was talking about," I muttered,

connecting the dots. "That was why Avra accused me of wanting to give our child to him."

Red rage surged within me, heating my blood and forcing me to step back and clench my teeth. I held my breath and attempted to temper the chaotic energy inside me and rein in my wrath to hear him as he continued.

"First of all, congratulations—"

"This is all hypothetical. Avra isn't with child," I snapped, trying not to direct my anger at him. He wasn't my target, but hearing him explain this plan made my blood boil.

He nodded. "Yes, sir."

"What else?"

Stephanos glanced toward the patio, checking for security. "A trust of over two hundred million Euros, potentially three hundred million, was established by Juno Vitalis for his daughters and remains intact. It can only be passed to a blood relative of the Vitalis family. Your father knew this since the coup. He arranged for the sisters' escape and intended to force your wife into marriage, but they vanished instead."

I shouldn't have been surprised. Ozias's greed knew no bounds. After all, didn't history love to repeat itself? He'd murdered Eudora. What was one more Vitalis woman? Or all of them? And why not add forcing a fifteen-year-old girl to marry a twenty-five-year-old, too?

"Tell me all of it."

"The land is legally divided among the sisters. Regardless of current claims, it won't belong to anyone while a Vitalis lives. Any child you have inherits everything. That's your father's plan. By taking your child, he gains control of the trust and land."

"You did well, Stephanos."

"There's more, sir."

I waited, knowing whatever he added would only fuel a storm inside me.

"We found a recruit with videos from our last meeting. He was on overwatch that day. Our team confiscated all of his belongings."

I clenched my jaw. "Where is he?"

"In holding."

"Did he tell you why he decided to record us?"

"To gain favor with your father, he believed the recording would prove his loyalty."

"Then how did it get to my wife?"

"That, I cannot say."

I'd find out up close and personal once I dealt with the old man.

"Go to Carlo. He is outside. He'll give you instructions. Be ready."

I waited to collect myself once I was alone.

I'd come here seeking answers, the details Avra had refused to share. Now I knew and understood the devastation on my beautiful wife's face.

No wonder she found it so hard to believe me. I wouldn't have believed me.

I stormed outside, squinting in the bright sunlight glaring in the cloudless sky. Scanning the crowd, I followed the robust sounds of deep laughter.

There. I found him. Ozias sat on a plush lounger, two young women sitting beside him and fawning over him. He relaxed in a loose white shirt with his arms around them both. In one hand, he held a lit cigar, smoke bellowing from the tip. With the other, he trailed his fingers along the top edge of one of the women's shirts, nearly exposing her breasts to all the people around them.

She tittered and giggled, sliding against him to cuddle and whisper something in his ear.

"Oh?" He chuckled, then furrowed his brow as I stalked closer.

I stood tall and unmoving, blocking out the sun. Casting him in my shadow, I hoped he felt the chill of the darkness, of my darkness, because ice ran in my veins at the sight of him out here like this.

Gluttonous with food on platters, indulging in underage whores. Smoking his cigars and joking with his chiefs. Like a fucking king.

"Son." His lips curled into a mocking half-smile as he reached forward and picked up his cocktail glass, complete with an olive on a stick. "Welcome home."

With his hand still outstretched, the cocktail liquid glistening with condensation, I fumed and tried to find my last reserve of patience.

I had none. His smug, mocking smile was all it took for me to react. Saying nothing, I reached forward and slapped his glass to the patio.

"Get out."

I ordered it once as the glass shattered and flew out in an arc from the stone slabs underfoot.

Music stopped. I felt the eyes of all the chiefs directed my way.

"Get. Out!"

They scrambled, climbing out of their chairs and leaving. The women seated with Ozias hurried away too, dodging any contact with the shards of glass. I'd come to a party scene of them all kicking back and living it up, and now, it was just me and him.

I didn't move, blocking the sun from touching him and warming him. I felt no warmth or benevolence for him. He didn't—hadn't ever—deserved it. Not from me. Not from anyone.

"I demand an explanation for your plan."

He pursed his lips together, feigning concentration, and he hummed. "What plan?"

"Don't fuck with me."

He chuckled. The sound grated on my nerves as he smirked at me like this was some big joke—an epic stunt.

"What plan? I have lots of plans, Eli. I'm the head of the Xenos Family. A leader has to have plans."

"You're not a leader."

His smile dimmed.

"You're nothing but a figurehead, an outdated example of what this family used to represent."

He pulled his lower lip in and bit it. Anger was creeping over his face, slowly, but he was losing the war to hide it from me. "And what did the family 'used' to represent?"

"Power."

He pointed at me, his cigar still wedged between his fingers. "Now, that, I agree with. The Xenos name used to be so readily associated with power."

Keep believing that. It had never been his to have in the first place.

"I said I want an explanation for your plans."

Reverting to the humor, he smiled and nestled back in his chair, puffing on his cigar. "I don't know what you're talking about."

Here we were once again. History repeated itself, with me pushing Ozias for answers and to own up to his schemes.

Not even an hour ago, I was at home with Avra, put on the spot just like I was putting Ozias on the spot. The only difference was that I was clueless when confronted with an accusation of participating in something I'd never heard about.

Ozias, on the other hand, was the mastermind of the entire conspiracy. He acted innocent when he was guilty of all this chaos.

"What is it? You're already so sick of married life that you want to return home?"

This place was never home. Not mine. Not his either, when he had to steal it from Juno Vitalis.

"It's tough, isn't it?" He puffed his cigar again. "Married life is a hassle. Listening to the wife bitch and nag. Wanting this and that. I can only imagine how fucking miserable that girl is making you."

I stood there and said nothing, letting his pathetic words

go in one ear and out the other. Who gave a damn what he felt about marriage? He never honored the one he had with his nonstop affairs.

The longer I remained silent, glaring down at him, the more he grew uneasy, squirming beneath my intense scrutiny.

His smile faded, then crumpled completely. His eyes narrowed as suspicion and annoyance claimed his mood. He shifted in his seat, unable to maintain eye contact.

Since childhood, the best way to irritate and push his buttons was with an unblinking stare and an added lack of response. He'd never been able to handle a silent treatment well. He couldn't take the suspense.

The only way he ever won this challenge was through physical violence. A child was no match for an adult. Of course, a slap to the face or a punch to the gut garnered a sound or reaction.

Now, as an adult, he knew better. If he dared to touch me, the hospital was where he'd end up.

"I don't understand why you're so angry, Eli." He shook his head, snarling as he tried to be more conversational. "You just said it yourself. We lost our power."

"It was never your fucking power." I slammed my fist to the table, cracking the glass top. It webbed, splitting into thick, pointed shapes. Each one of them became another weapon I could use on him, another sharp blade I could hold against his neck and end him.

Over the shattered table, I spilled what I'd heard. I shared what Avra had discovered. I repeated what Stephanos had just confirmed, never exposing him as the source. I laid it all out, heat coating my every word. The summary would be the same, no matter how I paraphrased it.

"Once I get Avra pregnant, you intend to eliminate the sisters for good. And after my wife gives birth, you want to get rid of her, too. Then, my son or daughter is the only living heir to the Vitalis trust and lands. Let me know if I have this right or wrong. You orchestrated the coup, the murders, everything from the very beginning for money?"

Silence hung between us, broken only by the tinkling trickle of water in the fountain across the patio. It didn't distract me. Nothing would interrupt my focus on the devil himself.

At last, he caved to the pressure of the quiet, losing this waiting game as well.

"For money, land, and power. You think too small, boy." Ozias shrugged. "What about it? That is how things run in our world."

I cracked my knuckles, fisting my hands so hard. He wasn't even going to try to deny it. He wasn't arguing or making excuses to get out of this. He'd all but owned up to the fact that this was his plan.

"You knew about everything when you went after Eudora and Juno."

"Of course I did. No one runs an operation like that without finding out every detail. You need to learn from my example." Ozias narrowed his eyes. "It's time to stop fucking around and become my son the way I raised you."

The way he fucking what?

"And what is it you expect of me?" I refused to hide my hatred.

"Get rid of the Vitalis girls."

My heart raced. He was out of his mind.

"One by one."

I couldn't even picture it.

He leaned forward, stubbing his cigar on a cracked piece of the table. "I've set part of the plan in motion. You will fall in line and end the 'figurehead' bullshit. Is that clear?"

"Cancel it." I set my teeth together so hard that they clacked.

He arched one brow. "Cancel what?"

"Cancel the hits." I stepped forward once, glad that he flinched. "Cancel the hits on them. Right. Fucking. Now."

He shook his head. "I won't."

"You better."

"It's a done deal."

I tried steadying my breaths. The vision of lunging at him and slamming my fist into his face was too tempting. I'd beat him to a pulp and relish every gasping and dying breath he'd wheeze out.

"I won't be a part of anything that brings more blood to those women."

His laughter made my cheek twitch. I'd never been so high-strung, so pushed with the viral need to inflict pain as I was now. Hearing him laugh like I was ridiculous was one taunt too far.

"Pathetic. That goddamn Vitalis pussy is making you

weak. So she's that good at it? Huh? She good at fucking you while she tries to fuck me over?"

I shook, coiled, and braced to attack.

"I should have known you'd turn out like your mother."

I slit my eyes, boring him with a lethal stare. "What?"

Under his breath, he muttered, "I'll never forget how happy I was when that bitch finally died."

I shuddered, overwhelmed with need to destroy this vile man. For that comment about my mother. About me. But most of all, about the wife I loved.

Killing him would be too fucking easy. It would be too quick of a reward. Besides, I knew his death belonged to Avra. She should be the one to end this piece of shit. It was time to throw this fucker off his throne.

Instead of launching at Ozias, I tipped my head. The guards surrounding us hadn't left. They were always there, waiting and watching, blended into the background.

I caught the eye of the leader, who was focused on me. I gestured forward, flicking my fingers in a come-hither motion. I directed him to surround my genetic donor, the man I hated from the deepest depths of my soul.

Ozias Xenos would finally learn the majority of the Xenos men only answered to me, not him. They hadn't taken orders from him in over a decade.

The soldiers moved forward as the trained unit they were and surrounded Ozias.

"What the fuck is this?" He shouted his outrage and moved his head from side to side, looking at them all.

"Stand down. Stop. I said stop!" His voice rose as he

stood, stunned in furious disbelief. "Make them stop. Stand the fuck back!"

They tightened the circle, blocking off any chance of escape. I remained where I stood, watching, assessing, and enjoying the show.

"I order you to stand back. What the fuck are you doing? Listen to me!" His face was pinched with anger, red and sweating as he bellowed useless instructions none of them followed.

Two of them grabbed him, securing him in their grasps and sending him down to his knees with deft kicks and confident maneuvers for holding a prisoner. He struggled, cursing and spewing spittle as he demanded that they release him.

Satisfied to see him on his knees, captured, and learning the true strength of his power, I watched as he puffed and bucked, frantic to get free. I wouldn't let them kill him. Not yet. Not until he spoke and told me all the details of the hits he'd put on Avra's sisters. On her.

"You won't win," he spat, snarling at me. "Even if you take over completely, you won't win."

I raised my brows, amused he'd still cling to his insane beliefs.

"We'll see," I replied, turning to leave. It was past time to return to Avra. I'd bring her here and show her how I'd captured him. We'd work together to torture him and get the details out of him about the hits on her sisters.

"Before you go," he sneered, breathing heavily from the exertion of his struggles, "I'm curious."

I stopped, not turning back to face him as I listened.

"Does your wife know where her dear baby sister is?"

I whipped around, catching sight of his sinister smirk.

Everything in me froze. My heart stopped, then thudded into overdrive. My lungs drew in shallow pants as panic kicked in.

Calista? No. She is too young. Too soft. Too gentle.

I could only hope it wasn't too late to save her.

TWENTY-FIVE

vra

"Where's the garlic?" Laya asked, pretending to gag after taking the first bite of her sandwich.

I wadded a napkin and tossed it at her face. "Oh, shut up."

"It's so plain. We're Greek. Give me flavor." She gestured with her hands and gave me a goofy smile that had me returning one.

"You can't taste anything because you burned all your taste buds with all the spicy food you eat. Normal people don't pick peppers from a plant in the garden and eat them."

"You weakling. You can't call it spicy if it doesn't make your nose run and your eyes water."

I rolled my eyes, took a huge bite of my food, and immediately regretted it. Hot cheese scalded my tongue.

I fanned my mouth and grabbed my cold soda. "Hot, hot, hot."

"I rest my case." Laya laughed, pointing at me.

"You're lucky I'm willing to feed you. I've never known anyone who eats as much as you." My comment brought thoughts of Cali to mind, and I glanced at my phone. "Has it really been three hours?"

Laya picked up her mobile and snapped her gaze to mine. "Where the hell is Cali?"

"Has she responded to any of your messages? She hasn't read any of mine." A chill ran down my spine. Cali always responded to texts, even if it was to say, *I'm busy.*

"Nothing." Laya scrolled her screen. "Not a single comment to any of the pictures I sent her while we were cooking. And not a single post on any of her social media accounts, even the popular one with the million followers."

Calista kept a "Day in the Life" account on one of the social media platforms where she posted about different places in the city. We teased her about the number of hand and foot shots we had seen since she never revealed her face.

I dialed her number. "Let me call. She knows to pick up if it is me."

After a few rings, her chirpy voice told me to leave her a message.

"Voicemail?" Laya asked. "Okay. I'm scared. Calista doesn't go this long without checking in. She's a free spirit but a good girl. She's not like us."

"Where the fuck is her protection?" I muttered to myself and dialed Cali's security lead. When he picked up, I asked, "Where's Cali?

"We can't find her."

I gripped the phone tighter. "What the fuck do you mean you can't find Cali? It's your job to keep her safe and to stay with her. You are her shadow."

Laya furrowed her brow, gesturing to listen in. My hands shook as I set the phone on the counter. It was time to be the Vitalis, to take charge, and to help my family through this.

I would use rational thought, and then I'd punish.

"Tell me what happened." My order came from a place I'd reached for before.

I remember Papa telling me there were times we put everything away and became cold and a predator. At fifteen, I had no concept of what he meant. Now I understood.

"She went into the library's enclosed study room. Since some of the walls are glass, she was within sight to a certain extent. So we stood nearby to give her some privacy to concentrate."

"She told us she was going to an information session."

"This was after it finished. There are books in the library that they won't allow anyone to check out, so Cali decided to look through them before closing. We didn't see any harm in letting her sit in a lounger and read for half an hour."

Laya cut in. "A single study room? She was the only one in there?"

"No. Several other tables were in there, but only one

other woman was there," he reported. "We scoped it before she entered."

"Go on." I set my hand on the counter and waited.

"When the thirty-minute time slot ended, we knocked on the door, but the room was empty."

I ground my teeth so hard that the muscles in my neck strained. The air in my lungs burned with every breath. Laya covered her mouth, rubbing her hand to the side to grip the back of her neck.

I couldn't lose the heart of our family. I wouldn't lose the heart of our family.

"We were about to call you, then Elias."

Laya glanced at me as though to ask whether I thought that was a good idea.

To the best of the men's knowledge, the Vitalis and Xenos forces were a unified group. No one was informed about the recent developments in my relationship with Elias.

I was confident that if the men had contacted my husband and reached him before me, he would have stepped in to help. I was confident he would do everything possible to locate Cali.

My soul said he'd help.

Was I a fool to believe this?

My arms and legs ached with the restrained anger building inside me. I wanted to lash out and rip into the soldier for failing at his one fucking duty.

But he was the last of my priorities. Calista came first.

Every bit of the chaotic, raging energy churning inside me needed to focus on finding Cali.

Laya's eyes locked with mine. Anger boiled within them, matching mine. She stood at my side, speechless and brimming with the urgency to do something. She kneaded her fingers in a clawing rub on the back of her neck.

"Contact Vik right now, and don't you dare stop searching. Your life depends on it." I hung up.

Not a second later, my cell vibrated with an incoming call flashing Eli's number.

"Eli," I said with every emotion rushing around me.

"Avra. Are you home? Are you safe?"

I hesitated, desperate to tell him about Calista, needing him so much.

He spoke before I could. "Calista was taken."

I shut my mouth so hard my teeth rattled. He knew? How—

"Ozias is behind it," he finished without me asking, reading my mind somehow.

"No." I swallowed hard, wishing it was just a fluke—a coincidence. I truly believed that Elias would prevent anything from happening.

"I promise you, I will do everything I can to get her back. I swear it."

How can I believe you? I thought he had gone over there to do this very thing and stop his father.

"Where is Ozias?"

He didn't hesitate to reply. The deep growl of his car sounded in the background as he revved to drive faster. "Locked in a secure room. Guards are monitoring his every move. He's not going anywhere."

"What does this mean?"

"There is no figurehead anymore. I am one hundred percent in power now."

Those words gave me a kernel of hope.

With Eli in charge, Ozias couldn't continue his plot against me and my sisters.

It still wouldn't make any difference to Cali.

"I will be home in a few minutes. Please, wait for me before you do anything."

Please. It wasn't an order but a request.

"Okay. I'll wait." I nodded, not caring if he could see the gesture or not.

I disconnected, the numbness after the incident with Eli nothing compared to the cold, ice-filled wrath surging through every one of my cells. Fury ate me from the inside out, burning out the pettier issues like heartache and confusion. Having already been torn and chewed up from the ups and downs of so many big emotions, it was time to unleash the hard, icy woman so many had labeled me.

I couldn't break.

I had a long to-do list—killing Ozias Xenos at the top of it. The need to punish him and inflict pain filled my mind. I envisioned killing him with my bare hands, shaking the life out of him as I strangled him and watched his eyes gloss over with death. Maybe I'd play with him first, torture him, then end his life.

I now had the opportunity. With Elias's update, I knew I could move forward. As an additional assurance, a few of

Vik's Vitalis spies, concealed among Ozias's men, confirmed everything Elias had conveyed to me.

Ozias was under lock and key, confined and surrounded, kept like prey awaiting his fate.

Yes, I chose to believe Eli and have faith in his intentions. However, Vik was always Vik, and when it came to his girls, it was a matter of "trust but verify." I couldn't blame him. He had played the role of a surrogate father for most of my life, and that wasn't going to change anytime soon.

A small part of me wondered why Elias hadn't done the deed himself, but now, a dark and malicious morsel of my soul was happy he hadn't. *I* wanted to end that bastard's existence. I wanted his blood on my hands.

No one would stop me. I could go there, open the door, and the soldiers could hold him still while I executed him however I saw fit.

But I couldn't do it. It would be wrong. Yes, Ozias deserved to die. Ozias would die, but not right now.

My time and efforts were needed elsewhere before it was too late.

Papa and Mama would understand avenging them came second to protecting my sisters.

My sisters mattered more. They always would.

Laya paced near me, and as she spun, mumbling under her breath, I faced her and met her worried gaze.

It was also time to accept the truth and blame our current circumstances on the right person.

"It's my fault Ozias took Cali."

She frowned, shaking her head. "No."

"If we'd stayed in Prague, none of this would have happened." I hung my head for a moment. "I failed her. I failed you."

"No!" She hurried over to me, taking hold of my upper arms. "That's not true. That's bullshit. All we had there was a life of looking over our shoulders and worrying while we hid. That's not a real life. At least not according to me."

I tugged out of her hold, unable to listen to anything else she argued.

The front door opened and shut, announcing Elias's return. I rushed out of the kitchen and stopped in the entryway.

We stared at each other. I didn't want to wonder or second-guess anything.

This man, my husband, vowed that he loved me. I should hate him. His father destroyed my childhood, killed my mother, and took my sister. But Eli wasn't like Ozias.

He wanted me, not my name or what I came with, but me.

"Eli," I whispered and ran to him.

He caught me, wrapping his arms around me and engulfing me in strength and security.

He released a deep, heartfelt sigh into my hair and pressed his face to my head. "I can't lose you, Avra. I can't."

"I should have believed you. I was—"

Eli placed a finger to my lips.

"If I heard just half of what Ozias planned, I'd question myself too."

"I'm scared." My admission felt like acid in my throat.

He lifted me in his arms and held me close. "They took Calista before I reached the estate."

"I know." I nodded and then said, "Tell me what happened."

He carried me to the couch and shared all the details with Laya and me. From the moment he arrived at the estate, where he learned from the guard about the talkative recruits, which corroborated Laya's account, to the events during Ozias's party.

"I could have killed him. I wanted to," he admitted, taking my hand. "But I couldn't deprive you of that satisfaction."

"Oh, isn't it sweet? He's giving you the top kill on your hit list as a present," Laya cooed, and I narrowed my gaze at her.

Instead of commenting on Laya's stupid words, I stated, "He lives until he reveals Calista's location."

Laya nodded. "And the details about the hits on us."

"Ozias won't crack easily. Plus, we need to find out what else he plans," Eli added.

"I don't care about Ozias right now." The anxiety inside me bubbled up again. "We need to use our time and resources to find Calista."

Eli turned me to face him on the couch and took my hands. "I want to make this clear and know that you understand me."

I waited for him to continue.

"Our marriage is real, Avra."

I stared into his intense eyes, seeing the true meaning behind his claims.

"It started as a business, an arrangement. We were openly using each other."

I smirked. "That we were. I remember something about actions and consequences."

His lips curved at my response, but then he grew serious.

"I love you, Avra." He slid his hand around my neck until he cupped the back of my head. "I will never stop loving you."

I drew in an unsteady breath and nodded.

"I swear to you, we will find Calista. I will do everything in my power to make it happen."

I let his firm words settle into my frantic thoughts.

"I believe you."

He crushed his mouth to mine, stealing thoughts and overwhelming my senses. And just as fast as he captured my lips, he pulled away. Anything more would come later.

I stood, still holding his hand and squeezing his fingers as he rose.

"I'll call Vik and see what he can figure out."

Elias nodded once. "I'll start with Ozias. Time to give him a taste of his own medicine and see if we get some answers."

"Make it hurt, Eli." I held his gaze as his pupils dilated, and that attraction that lived as if it were a sentient being called out.

"The two of you can eye fuck later. We have work to do."

Twenty-Six

E lias

"I fucking hate you," I muttered to myself and gripped my hair. "Where did you hide, Calista? Where did you fucking go?"

Two weeks of calling in every favor possible, and nothing. Not a damn thing.

Calista must have fallen off the face of the earth because of how well her kidnappers hid her.

Either that or—

No. I shook my head. I refused to believe Calista was dead.

No matter what my pragmatic side said, I couldn't stop looking.

On top of everything, Ozias had escaped by nightfall on the same day I'd taken over the Xenos family. We lost several of my loyal guards, who told me someone from the inside worked against us. Then early the following day, we found those traitors with their throats slit.

Laya confirmed that they were some of the men from the bar. My father had killed them as a precaution, just in case I got my hands on them.

Vik and I combed through the Xenos men, searching for answers and any other rat, but none knew anything.

Ozias had disappeared, depriving us of a chance to get answers from him.

The Xenos and Vitalis men investigated every rumor and whisper linked to Ozias or Calista, but all we found were dead ends.

Then, there was Avra's family in Boston. They blamed me for everything. I accepted their accusations. I hadn't protected the sisters as was my duty. Now, their forces searched alongside ours.

I'd failed my wife.

The only positive in this fucking mess was the world understood the Xenos and Vitalis families were a united front, and our common enemy was Ozias Xenos.

I glanced at my mobile, willing it to ring. Why wouldn't they call? I was tired of waiting.

My desperation reached such a high or low that I contacted the northern Italians. To my surprise, they welcomed my call. Now, I had to wait for them to extend whatever assistance they planned to offer.

The fucking politics of things never stopped. But if it meant finding Calista, I'd do it.

Her absence was tearing our lives apart. Avra and Laya were losing their minds, and the hope for a happy outcome diminished in their eyes with each passing hour.

I had to make it right.

I wasn't the one who'd orchestrated this, but it was my father who caused them this heartache.

I would bear the guilt for not keeping a closer eye on Ozias for the rest of my life. I knew he was the worst of humanity, and I shouldn't have allowed anything to shake my vigilance to know his every move.

My gaze locked on the picture I kept of Avra on my desk. It was a candid shot from our wedding day. She bore the type of beauty written about in mythology, natural, unapologetic, and in your face.

Shadows lay heavy under her eyes now from lack of sleep and days upon days of worry. Avra wasn't one to show her emotions to others, except in this case, the woman I loved was so desperate to find her sister that anyone who looked her way saw the fear of the possible outcome.

My cell phone rang, and I grabbed it, answering, "Xenos."

"Mia stigmí, kýrie."

Did he say, "One moment, sir, in Greek?" I fucking asked for the Italians.

I waited on the phone, pacing faster, wanting to know what the fuck was going on.

Then it dawned on me. The Italians were related to

Nikolas Galanis. He ran a territory in the south rivaling the size of the territory Juno Vitalis once owned. Having his help as a Greek and an Italian was an offer I couldn't turn down.

Nikolas Galanis was a hard man, according to the reports I'd found, but that didn't matter. He could be a fucking asshole so long as he helped me find Avra's sister. Manners were overrated.

"Xenos," he answered as a greeting.

"Thank you for stepping in to assist us." Okay, perhaps manners did matter at times. I wouldn't kiss anyone's ass, but I'd ensure he grasped how serious this situation was.

"I've heard about your efforts to locate a woman-your wife's cousin?" There were noises on his side of the call.

"Sister. My wife's sister."

"Yes. She is a cousin to my cousin's wife."

Instead of commenting, I said, "Do you have information on her?"

"I've had my men on the streets in Athens. Some of them have been reporting rumors of a high-value product."

I tensed, gripping my phone tighter. Already, this sounded promising. "Any more details?"

"A woman confined in a basement in a high-traffic neighborhood."

My pulse skyrocketed. I didn't want to get my hopes up, but—

"Fuck, I am glad you have men in the area."

"I have men everywhere." He chuckled wryly. "From what my men have heard, they think it might be a Vitalis."

Athens? I was flying there immediately. "Can you get closer?"

"Of course." He paused to listen to some conversation in the background. "The property I mentioned belongs to what we call freelancers. And they confirm a woman is with them."

I gritted my teeth and closed my eyes.

Freelancers. Guns for hire were what they were. They pledged no loyalty to any family and followed no formal structure. They worked for a paycheck.

He spoke some more with his men. I heard him give directions about discretion and call up others in the area as backup.

My heart hammered in my chest as thoughts of what they could have done to Calista came to mind. How would I tell Avra any of this? I wouldn't hide any details from her, but this wasn't good.

Avra was strong. She tried to take it in stride, but she would break inside. At least she knew Cali was alive instead of succumbing to the worst-case scenario.

When Nikolas returned, he instructed, "Meet me at my estate outside Athens."

"Done," I said. Athens wasn't too far.

"I'll be waiting," he replied, telling me when to call back.

Just as we prepared to hang up, he shouted, stopping me. "Hold on. Hold on. Xenos? Elias! Are you there?"

"Yes." I hadn't disconnected yet. "Yes, I'm here."

"Get ready to fly. We'll wait for you to raid, but I can confirm it's your sister-in-law. Calista Vitalis." Papers shuffled from his end of the call. "One of my men managed to grab a picture of the woman tied to a chair."

I swallowed. "Alive?"

He grunted. "Barely. Beaten and bloody, but comparing the girl to the picture we found online, it's her."

"We're on our way."

I hung up, running inside to tell Avra.

"Avra!" I sprinted toward our room.

Laya had just woken from a nap on the couch, and she was startled so much that she rolled right off to the floor, muttering and mumbling as she snapped, "Cali?"

"Avra!" I pushed open the door, catching her in the middle of a workout.

She stared at me, sweat dripping down her face. Her lips quivered, and I nodded.

"Let's go."

Her eyes went wide. "You found her?"

"Yes, in Athens." I grabbed her hand as we hurried out the door.

She remained at my side during the flight. Her excitement and determination to get to Cali rejuvenated her.

Laya and Avra bombarded me with question after question, barely taking a breath between them. I gave them the unfiltered truth, sparing them no detail, warning them of all the scenarios we could walk into.

Meeting Nikolas was a brief blur of formal greetings. He was all about business, helping us get near the area they'd been scoping. Since it was his turf, and he knew the lay of the land, I deferred to his lead. We kept our men to a minimum, and before too long, we positioned ourselves outside the warehouse where his man had taken a picture through the window of the woman bound inside.

"You stay back," I ordered Avra and Laya before we got too close.

This was the moment we'd been waiting for. We'd lost sleep and appetites, too full of worry over Calista's fate for so long.

We couldn't screw it up now.

Not if Avra insisted on being the hero and distracting me with anxiety about *her* safety, too. She was a bold, badass fighter. I knew this. But I was also painfully aware of the mental toll this had taken on her. She wasn't as sharp as she could be, too jittery with the need to protect her sister. She wasn't as alert and logical, operating with a precise reaction time. Instead, she moved, emphasizing her emotions: rage and impatience.

We couldn't risk sloppy work. We all had to be at our best to get Calista out of there alive.

"Avra, you stay—"

She shot me a stern look. "Tell me what to do again and see what I do to you."

Laya moved right up next to Avra and braced herself to creep closer until the scout signaled the all-clear to bust through the windows and doors.

Fuck.

She wasn't going to listen. Why was I surprised?

The second we got the signal, she went in with Laya, guns drawn.

I followed them, trying to remain as close to them as possible.

We would get Cali back, making it one small part of my repentance for all the ways I'd failed them because of Ozias.

If given the chance, I would kill every last one of those fuckers who'd touched Cali.

Nikolas narrowed his gaze as he focused on Laya before giving instructions to his men, who gathered closer to Avra and Laya.

I waited for Avra to say something, but in the next second, someone burst through the basement entrance of the building, and everyone's attention homed in on the task at hand.

Soldiers blocked all exits, and soon, all that rang out around us were the sounds of gunshots, the breaking of furniture, and shouts from fighting. A battle of trained killers and skilled fighters ensued.

A murderous haze filled my mind, and I stalked straight to the area where I knew the fuckers held Cali. I gunned down anyone who got in my way and all who targeted Avra as she charged in the same direction.

My heart stuttered, almost stopping with the stark realization that one of the assassins grinned as if he recognized Avra and pointed his weapon at her head.

Fuck, no. The thought of losing Avra sent me into a frenzied rage, increasing my speed and accuracy. I emptied my clip relentlessly, taking out every threat targeting her without hesitation. Avra pushed through the door before her, pivoted, and fired straight at the man standing next to Calista. Laya took out the tall brute holding guard behind the door.

And there she was, bound and bleeding, tied to a chair. Her torn, tattered clothes draped off her petite frame, and her head hung low. There wasn't a way to see if she was breathing.

Avra kneeled before her and pressed her fingers to Cali's pulse point.

"Dead?" one of Nikolas's men asked.

"Unconscious," Avra replied as she cut the ropes holding her youngest sister captive.

For the next few minutes, she concentrated on freeing her hands while I cut at the rope around her ankles.

She glanced up at me, tears glossy in her green eyes, and whispered, "Thank you. Thank you for finding her."

I stared into her eyes, knowing it was far from over. My father was still out there, and I would never earn gratitude there.

"I will *always* keep my promises," I reminded her as Cali slumped forward, free.

I picked her up, ready to carry her somewhere secure so she could receive medical attention. As I adjusted her fragile, too-light weight in my arms in a fireman hold, hurrying before anyone came back here or fired again, I pulled Avra close to my side and kissed the top of her head.

My wife would always come first.

And saving her sister was part of the package I was glad to have for the rest of my life.

There was nothing I wouldn't do for her in the name of love.

TWENTY-SEVEN

Elias

I sat on the patio, gazing at the distant waves as the sun sank, readying to kiss the horizon and disappear.

Brooding and dwelling, I failed at this so-called relaxation. I wouldn't forget about how we'd gotten into this mess.

Ozias was still out there, adjusting his plans and setting the rest into action. I refused to call his bluff, not when they were hits on my wife and her sisters.

Still, I wanted to sit and calm down for at least a few hours for the rest of the night. We'd succeeded in finding Cali. She lived. And Ozias couldn't evade me forever.

One day at a time, Eli. One day at a time.

Calista faced a long road to recovery. She had remained in and out of consciousness until we finally managed to get her to a private medical facility Nikolas oversaw.

However, once her mind cleared, her eyes were filled with fear and unimaginable horror. There wasn't any need to confirm what she'd endured, I knew.

If they hadn't been dead already, I'd take great pleasure in making them wish for death.

We returned to Patras immediately. We set Calista up with round-the-clock care of doctors and nurses in the guest wing of the house. With rest and physical rehabilitation, she would make a full recovery.

Mentally? I had no idea.

Her scars ran deep and jagged. I would find a way to help her, even if it meant flying in the best therapist in the world to counsel her.

I exhaled deeply, attempting to let go of the tension I had carried for weeks. For one night, at least, I could say I'd delivered on a promise I had made.

I wasn't like Ozias Xenos at all. He knew nothing of love except for a love of himself.

There was no understanding him, and trying to do so was an exercise in futility. It was better to focus on the peace I felt for the first time in my life.

I watched the birds dive into the waves and lift back into the air.

Was this what it felt like to have a home?

As if my thoughts had conjured her, the rustle of Avra's nightgown alerted me to her arrival.

"I thought you were going to bed," I said.

She glided over the stone, and her hair flew in gloriously long, dark tresses over her shoulders and down her back with the breeze. As she walked closer, I noticed the lingering sadness in her eyes and the fatigue on her beautiful face.

"I couldn't stop thinking." I opened my arms, and she snuggled against me. "I want to take Cali's pain away. But it isn't possible."

I nodded, brushing my lips over her temple.

She burrowed against me as if she couldn't get close enough.

She fit.

She was so tall, so much larger than life with her spirit and strength, but in these private moments, I cherished how delicate and small she seemed compared to me. It reminded me of her reliance on me, how she counted on me for my strength and guidance, and I'd never forsake her for ever needing them.

"She'll have such a long road ahead of her," she said.

"She will. And we won't let her do it on her own."

"You don't mind if she moves in here?"

I shook my head. "Whatever she wants, I'll make it happen."

She leaned up and cupped my face, kissing my cheek.

"I have no doubt she'll survive it all," I told her. "I've realized the Vitalis women are stronger than they look."

"Hmmm." She rubbed her cool hand over my chest. "We are."

"Not to mention their sharpshooter skills."

She lifted her head and grinned.

"Who taught you?"

"Papa."

"He'd be proud of you, you know."

She peered up at me. "Did you ever meet him?"

"Once, without knowing who he was. I spoke with him at a meeting."

"I'm sure he would've come around to appreciate you as his son-in-law. You're not so bad when you're not mean."

I arched a brow. *"Mean?"*

"You look pretty good while you're at it. I like it when you're rough."

I held her closer, dragging my hand up her thigh and savoring her soft yet firm warmth.

"I see how it is. You like the dirty side of me better than the elegant side."

She toyed with her lip, pulling it between her teeth for a second. It drove me crazy, tempting me to lower my head and kiss her bite away. "I love all sides of you."

I gripped her thigh, loving the sound of those words on her lips. It wasn't the first time she'd told me, but it was the first time since Ozias had imploded my world. I had nearly lost her because of him. I'd believed I would never hear her say those words to me again.

I couldn't look away, staring at her soulful, sweet gaze.

"Say it again."

"I love all sides of you."

I growled, diving in to kiss her perfect lips. She wrapped

her arms around my neck as I stood, picking her up and carrying her back into our room.

"Again."

"This isn't something new. I've said this before." She almost giggled, smiling up at me.

"I like hearing it. Now say it."

"I love you."

I toppled to the bed, still kissing her and holding her close on top of me.

"Again—"

"You're so silly." Her hands gripped my pants, shoving them down.

She rolled with me as I positioned her beneath me. "Only you would ever say such a thing to me. I'm mean and a killer."

"Definitely silly. I love you." She reached up to seal her parted lips over mine, dueling with my tongue.

Desire lanced through me, heightened and spiced with something extra as she repeated the words between kisses.

"I love the way you drive me crazy." She threaded her fingers through my hair as I lifted up to kick off my pants. Naked, I rolled her again so she'd be on top.

"I love the way you know how to fuck me." She tugged her nightgown off, gifting me the sweet reward of her tan, smooth, bare skin, all for me to feast on.

"No." I pulled her beneath me again, enjoying the light laughter that slipped out at our constant battle for who'd be positioned where. "How to fuck you?" I lowered, covering her with my body as I kissed her long and deep. She wrapped her arms around my back and locked her legs in a tight loop around my waist.

She moaned into my mouth, panting and breathing heavily as I lined my cock up to her wet pussy. I pushed the head in, stretching her as I rose to see her face.

"I don't mind fucking you," I said.

She rolled her eyes at my teasing tone.

"But this time." I thrust inside her with a long, hard push, winning her sexy moan in reply. "I want to make love to you, wife."

Her smile was slow and sweet, lost with mine as I kissed her and filled her with deliberately slow slides through her slick pussy. She gripped me like a glove, milking me too soon.

As the tension built along my spine, in my balls, seconds before I came, I cupped her chin and tipped her face up to mine. "I love you."

Her lips parted, caught in a silent groan as she came, squeezing me close, her trembling legs still hooked around my waist.

"Oh..." She opened her eyes after shutting them so tight at the release. "I love you, too, Eli." She smoothed her hand along my jaw. "Forever."

I collapsed onto her, then shifted to my side so we could lie together, catching our breath and watching the moon rise in the sky through the open doors.

As her chest rose and fell steadily and she drifted asleep, I closed my eyes. I held her close, content with the realization that I'd finally found my family in the arms of my enemy.

Ready to see how Laya takes on the Vitalis claim?

Then grab Influence and see how she navigates, fighting for her birthright and marriage to a man who hides a darker side behind the facade of a calm, always-in-control persona.

https://geni.us/InfluenceSiennaSnow

A marriage of convenience. A game of power. A love worth the risk.

Layana Vitalis has one goal: rebuild her family's empire. To succeed, she must marry her enemy—a man as dark and dangerous as the life she was born into.

Nikolas Galanis, a king in the Greek Mafia, demands respect and control in every aspect of his life. But from the moment they meet, Layana tests his limits in ways no one else has dared.

Beneath the façade of an arranged marriage lies a battle of

wills and forbidden desires. As their enemies close in and family secrets resurface, Layana and Nikolas must decide if their growing bond is strong enough to survive the darkness threatening to tear them apart.

In this gripping second installment of the Sisters of Wrath series, loyalty, passion, and power collide, proving love can be the deadliest weapon of all.

Perfect for readers who love arranged marriages with sizzling chemistry, lethal power dynamics, and morally grey heroes—fans of Natasha Knight, Rina Kent, and A. Zavarelli will devour **Influence**.

BOOKS BY SIENNA

Rules of Engagement

Rule Breaker

Rule Master

Rule Changer

Politics of Love

Celebrity

Senator

Commander

Gods of Vegas

Master of Sin

Master of Games

Master of Revenge

Master of Secrets

Master of Control

Master of Fortune

Sweetest Sin

Intrigued By Love

Street Kings

Dangerous King

Vicious Prince

Deceptive Knight

Ruthless Heir

<u>Violent Delights</u>

Claim

Defy

Own

<u>Sin and Lies</u>

Sin and Betrayal

Sin and Deception

<u>Sister of Wrath</u>

Legacy

Influence (June 6, 2025)

Power (June 27, 2025)

<u>Sinful Gods</u>

Forbidden Empire (Sept 3, 2025)

Dark Alliance (2026)

Broken Crown (2026)

<u>Collections</u>

Reckless Romeo

Take Me To Bed (2019)

Meet Me Under The Mistletoe (2021)

Nightingale (A charity anthology in support of Ukraine) - (2022)

Darkly Ever After (An Organized Crime Anthology) (2022)

RARE Melbourne Anthology (2023)

About the Author

USA Today bestselling author Sienna Snow loves to craft dark and extremely sexy stories centered on anti-heroes and the strong, unapologetic women who bring them to their knees. Her books immerse you in a world of indulgence, suspense, and undeniable steam.

Her heroines are vibrant and self-assured, often discovering love and romance under unconventional circumstances. Sienna offers her readers enticing glimpses of steamy romance filled with empowerment and indulgent satisfaction.

Sienna loves a life filled with travel and adventure. She plans to explore even the farthest corners of the world and revel in experiencing the diverse cultures along the way. When she isn't writing or traveling, Sienna is focused on her "happily ever after" with her husband and children.

Sign up for her newsletter for notifications of releases, book sales, events, and so much more.

http://www.siennasnow.com/newsletter

contact@siennasnow.com